CU00794457

Also by Emily Kazmierski

Ivory Tower Spies Series

For Your Ears Only
The Walk-in Agent (a Julep Short Story)
The Eyes of Spies
Spy Your Heart Out
Spy Got Your Tongue
Over My Dead Body (Coming July 2019)

Other Novels

Malignant
Life Among the Ashes
All-American Liars

Copyright © 2019 Emily Kazmierski
Cover Design: Mariah Sinclair

All rights reserved. This book or any portion thereof
may not be reproduced or used in any manner whatsoever
without the express written permission of the publisher
except for the use of brief quotations in a book review.
Printed in the United States of America

First Printing, 2019

ISBN: 978-1-7322435-4-5

www.EmilyKazmierski.com

SPY GOT YOUR TONGUE

IVORY TOWER SPIES BOOK FOUR

EMILY KAZMIERSKI

For my sister. Hi Erin!

Chapter 1

Adrenaline courses through me as I stretch my arms and legs. "You ready for this?" I whisper to Haru, who's crouching next to me, hands on her knees. Her face sets in grim determination. It's her first time in the field; I hope she rises to the challenge.

She reaches up with both hands to tighten her ponytail. "This isn't what I was expecting."

Clapping a hand on her shoulder, I meet her eyes with a serious look in my own. "You can do this. Just listen to what I tell you, and don't hesitate. No one gets left behind."

"That's right," Lotus says from her other side, his jaw set. "We're gonna kick some ass."

I glance at Clarity, who's standing on my left. She's tightening her shoe laces, ready to bolt once the signal is given.

A look over my shoulder gives me a glimpse of Julep and Starling, who are stretching to loosen up. Starling rolls his shoulders, ready for action.

I shake my head. Sometimes that guy is so good it's maddening. It's obvious why Royal recruited him to join our team of spies, based out of the Ivory Tower in Washington, D.C.

Thankfully, after my quick work in Sicily, I've been reinstated to the team. No more concierge work for me.

Starling looks great in his black athletic shorts and vivid blue tank top. He finishes his calf stretch and stands to full height, his eyes catching mine. A confident smile rises to his face at the sight of me staring.

I whip around to the front, my chest warm.

Clarity bumps me with her arm and raises an arched brow.

"What?" My fingers comb through my bleached blond hair, pushing it off my forehead.

Raising her other eyebrow to match the first, she leans toward me and whispers. "Should I be prepared for you to start sneaking off in the middle of the night?"

"No!" I snap, too loudly, and continue in a lower voice. "We barely know each other."

"But you're attracted to him."

I bite my lip. "Well, yeah."

She snorts. "You and secret agent men."

"Is there something wrong with that?" I ask in mock offense, hands on hips.

She gives a slow shake of her head, her stubby ponytail not moving from where it's fixed to the nape of her neck.

"I need someone who can handle all this." I wave over my entire body with one hand. "Some guys consider it a turnoff to date a girl who can kill them with a chopstick."

"And you have so much experience with guys," she retorts in a whisper.

"More than you."

All I get for this is an eye roll. "I'm perfectly content with my current inner circle, thank you."

A large hand presses into the small of my back. "Are you ladies ready?" Starling asks, inserting his head between Clarity's and mine.

My heart thumps at his nearness, but I will it to behave. Focus, Loveday. I clench my jaw. "Stick together. Help each other. We do this as one."

"Yes, ma'am," he says, the corner of his mouth ticking up in a cocky grin.

A gunshot rends the air. Chaos erupts around us as bodies surge forward, away from the shooter.

"Move!" I lunge forward through the early morning haze, my shoes squelching through the thick mud at our feet. A torrential midnight storm has made the ground soggy and slick. Flecks of dirt cling to my legs, harsh dark spots against my pale skin.

A ten foot wooden fence looms ahead. The first obstacle.

A man with a muscled arm elbows Lotus as he runs past, making Lotus twist out of the way, but his face remains focused.

"Ready?" I yell to my team.

"Yep," Lotus says. He and Starling move forward to the base of the wall. Starling knits his fingers together to make a cradle, and kneels. Mud streaks their legs as they move together in practiced formation.

Lotus steps into Starling's waiting hands, and Starling stands, propelling Lotus to the top of the wall. Once he's crested the peak, he lays flat on his stomach on the ledge, holding an arm down. "Next," he says. All of the time he's spent working out is about to pay off.

My heart pounds as, one by one, Starling hoists each of us up so we can grab Lotus's arm. Clarity, Haru, Julep, and I clamber over the wall.

Lastly, Starling takes a running leap and grabs Lotus's hand. Straining, Lotus pulls him up the side of the fence and heaves him onto the platform.

"Great. Now let's move!"

We throw ourselves down the giant metal slide on the other side, slicking our clothes with mud.

Up ahead, there's a laser array blocking our path.

The only way past the security measure is to crawl underneath.

Haru frowns, but kneels and pushes herself under, wriggling through the mire on her stomach.

Clarity and Julep follow, fanning out to either side of Haru's advancing form.

Turning, I scan the field, and catch sight of Starling, who is grinning from ear to ear.

"What are you so happy about?" I ask, not able to prevent the corner of my mouth from lifting.

He points at the ground with one finger. "This. This is what I live for."

"Crawling in the mud?" I tease.

"No." He shakes his head. "Doing something like this with our team, working together. It's… I've always wanted to feel like part of something. To feel like someone needs me." His eyes rise to mine.

"You're part of our team now," I say, my words measured.

He tilts his head, waiting to see if I'll say anything else.

"Shall we?" I ask, finally, gesturing toward the lasers.

"Ladies first," he says.

By the time we get past all of the obstacles, every one of us is covered head to toe in mud. It dries on my shoulders, crusting and crackling in the increasing heat of the day. Even my hair is slick with the muck where I've pushed it away from my face with dirt-caked fingers.

The only one who's managed to keep her face clean is Julep, and I have no idea how.

The warm, earthy scent fills my nostrils as we push toward our objective. Before us, a mud puddle that can only be described as a pool of filth blocks our path.

I go in first, lowering myself into the mire and slogging across, my legs pushing with the extra weight of my clothes and shoes in the thick sludge.

When I reach the other side, I pull myself out of the muck with steady hands and crouch at the edge, waiting for my teammates. I'll give them a hand out if they need it.

One at a time they hurl themselves into the muck, their willingness to follow me causing my heart to squeeze.

Haru is the last one across. She's clearly losing steam, her breath coming in gasps.

Clarity and I pull her out of the pool and stand her up in one motion.

"You can finish this," I say low in her ear. "We're almost done. Just one more mud puddle and we're there. Okay?"

A woman wearing an angry expression plows into me, almost knocking me flat. My instincts kick in and I use her momentum to fling her off me. She sprawls across the ground, landing flat on her back in the mud. "Hey!" she yowls. With a glare, I turn away from her.

Meeting Haru's eyes, I whisper. "Stay close."

Her head bobs, but she can't find the air to respond.

"All you have to do is give one more big push," Clarity says, "and you're done."

Haru smiles weakly. "Okay," she squeezes out between breaths. "Let's finish this." She stumbles forward, and we follow after her.

Beside me, Starling's body powers forward, his calf muscles straining.

To my other side, Julep's eyes are focused on the enemy combatants ahead of us, watching to make sure no one makes a move against us.

We're thirty yards away from our objective when Haru stops in her tracks in the middle of a large mud puddle. "My shoe!" she squeals.

"So close," Lotus says, fist clenched. He doubles back, wading to where she's standing.

Seconds tick by as he digs around in the mud.

A woman rushes Clarity from behind, sending her flying, her long limbs loose with surprise. At the last moment, she tucks and rolls, jumping into a squat, hands ready to defend herself.

The woman eyes her cautiously, probably evaluating her chances. She must not like her odds, because she takes a few steps back before bolting away from us.

"Found it," Lotus calls, holding up a blob that could possibly be a shoe. "Here."

Haru takes the thing in her hand and attempts to insert her foot, but it's no use.

"We're almost there," I say, my words clipped. "Leave the shoe."

After a mere flicker of hesitation, she drops it.

"Let's go!"

We move into the formation we practiced, Starling at the front, using his muscle to make a way through the throngs of people.

The tree line looms, marking our target.

With a last burst of adrenaline, we fling ourselves into the stand of trees, our shoulders heaving with effort.

Cheers go up from the waiting crowd.

My heart is hammering in my chest and my breath comes hard.

"That was great," Julep says, flinging her muddy arms around Clarity, and then turning to hug Lotus. Her arms linger around his shoulders for a split second longer before she pulls away. Sliding her arm around Haru's heaving frame, she rests her head against the younger girl's. "Congratulations. You just completed your first mud run. And you did great," she says. "Really. Fantastic."

Haru is panting, and her face is bright red. At least, the parts of it not covered in mud are. Even so, she smiles at Julep's words. "Thank you. It was… kind of fun."

We all burst out laughing, the adrenaline rushing through our veins.

"Britannia rules the waves!" Starling hollers, throwing his hands in the air.

Lotus guffaws.

"Shut up, pretty boy," I say, still chuckling.

He throws a wolfish smile my way. "You think I'm pretty?"

My eyes float skyward. "Oh, brother."

"Come on," he says, joining in Lotus's laughter. He gives me a quick side hug, and his body brushes against mine.

Clarity grins down at me. "My skin is going to be so soft once I get all this off." She gestures to the mud covering her from head to toe.

I shake my head, leading our team toward the portable showers set up at the edge of the clearing. Already there are long lines of participants waiting for their turn to hose themselves off.

"Think anyone will shoot at us today?" I quip.

At my side, Clarity's body tenses. "I hope not," she murmurs.

Concern needles at me. I open my mouth to respond, but Julep beats me to it.

"Don't worry, we're ready for it," she says, winking at us.

Beside Julep, Starling's head bobs in agreement. He's adjusted to our less rigorous schedule in record time.

But Clarity doesn't relax as we walk. Something's bothering her. I just don't know what.

Chapter 2

Buildings and trees rush past in a blur as Lotus drives into the city. Julep sits up front with him, whispering so the rest of us can't hear their conversation.

In the middle seat, Haru and Clarity are slouched together, dozing. The early morning call time was tough for both of them.

Beside me, Starling is working on another crossword puzzle.

My mind won't quiet.

It's been six weeks since we got home from Sicily, and something is still off with Clarity. Beppe Arnoni is in prison. So is my aunt Megan, who sold us out to the mob boss in an act of self-preservation. But somehow, my sister still doesn't feel safe.

Truthfully, I don't feel completely safe either. Nexus is still out there somewhere doing who knows what. If the CIA has any clue, they aren't sharing. I should be at ease knowing that they've got their top officers working on finding the guy, but I'm not. My team always seems to get roped into his nefarious plans, so it's just a matter of time before the other shoe drops. And it always does.

"Earth to Loveday."

I blink rapidly as Lotus's voice breaks into my reverie. "What?"

"We'll be there in five minutes." He steers the wheel with loose hands as we drive through the streets.

"Thanks." Giving myself a mental shake, I focus on the road ahead.

Starling's pinky brushes against my leg.

I glance at him through lowered lashes, and he grins.

My stomach flips. Even after six weeks, his touch still sends a shiver through me. We haven't talked about what we're doing, sneaking kisses in the spare moments we're not with the other members of our team, but I don't care. There's a sense of contentment between us that I rarely felt with Vale.

A lopsided smile rises to my lips. Whatever we're doing, it's fun.

My thoughts return to the mud run we completed this morning. My team worked beautifully together, like a well-oiled machine. Even Haru, who's never done any field exercises with us, fought like a champ through the muck. Even minus a shoe.

Excitement pushes me along the service tunnel and into our base, the Ivory Tower. I can't wait to give my dad a report of the morning. I think he'll be proud. "Royal?" I call.

No answer.

"See you in a few," I say to Clarity, whose body finally relaxes within the confines of our underground home.

"Okay," she says before retreating down the hall to the dormitory. She retrieves her cell from the front pocket of her clean sweatshirt, putting it to her ear as she enters our room.

Lotus, Starling, and Julep pile into the hall past me, pushing and shoving with playful movements, hoping to be the first ones to reach the bathrooms and the end of the hall.

Starling gives me a wink as he passes, making warmth pool

in my belly.

Renewed glee at my success pushes me through the den and down the hall into the control room. "Royal? Wait until you hear…" My voice halts.

My dad is in the control room, all right, but so is Charles Darnay.

I stiffen, eyes narrowing.

The man's eyebrows rise at the sight of my bedraggled, dirty clothes, but he quickly regains his composure. His lips part in what I assume is meant to be a charming smile from where he's standing near one of the front desks with Royal, examining a blueprint on the wall-sized screen at the front of the room.

I study it for a moment, not sure what I'm looking at. Then I turn my focus to the two men. "What's he doing here?" I blurt, eyeing Darnay with suspicion. "Got another job for us where you don't give us important details?"

Royal huffs. "That is no way to talk to a guest," he admonishes.

"Sorry," I say in a snide tone.

"I apologized for that… terrible incident in Kuala Lumpur," Darnay says, taking a step toward me.

My feet take an involuntary step back.

Darnay halts. "You don't trust me?" His smile widens. "Smart girl. But, alas, I'm not here with a job for you and your compatriots. Just visiting."

"You seem to be doing a lot of that lately."

His eyebrow rises at my cheek. "Yes, well…" His eyes skim over me, appraising me, before turning to Royal. It's a clear dismissal. "As I was saying…" he draws out the words, waiting for me to leave.

I don't move. Whatever Darnay is up to, I need to know. I

won't allow his carelessness to harm anyone else on my team. Not like the first time. And since it appears that Royal doesn't mind my presence...

My dad clears his throat. "Loveday."

"Yes?" I put on a winning smile.

"Was there a reason for your interruption?"

I grit my teeth. The pride I felt at our team's successful completion of the mud run landing ebbs away like steam rising off the streets in New York city. "No. Nevermind."

He studies me for a beat. "You're dismissed. Bring everyone back for a meeting in half an hour, all right?"

"Yes, sir." I spin on my heel and march out of the room, skimming my fingers along the underside edge of the large conference table as I go.

Once I'm in the hallway, the men's voices begin again, but they're an unintelligible murmur from where I'm standing. Disappointed, I join Clarity in our room.

"How's Uncle Nestore?"

Clarity smiles up at me from where she's sitting on the ground, peeling off her sodden socks. "He's great. He was telling me how it's going, legitimizing his business."

My eyebrow cocks. "And is it? Going, I mean?"

A hint of worry rests behind her eyes. "It's difficult, convincing the rest of the men that they'll all be better off once they're operating within their government's rules. Some of them rather liked it the way my grand—Beppe Arnoni ran things." Her eyes fall to her toenails, each painted a different shade of blue.

I sink onto the floor beside her, my knee bumping hers. After we got home from Sicily, Clarity begged Royal to let her remain in contact with her uncle. Her argument was that he had no idea of her background in espionage, and so wouldn't compromise her. When I saw the pleading look in her eyes, I knew our dad would agree to let her talk to her uncle, her only remaining biological tie to her mother.

Clarity's head lists toward mine, and she closes her eyes.

I can't help but wonder if she's imagining what it was like, being held in that room in the second story of the Arnoni house, but I don't ask. She acted so relieved after she'd walked us through her captivity that first time that I know she doesn't want to talk about it again.

Instead, I lick my lips. "Your uncle, he's a smart guy. He helped you escape, didn't he?"

Clarity's eyes flick up to mine, a hint of pink in her cheeks.

"He's going to be just fine."

She relaxes beside me, reassured.

Craning my neck to one side, I wait until I hear the pop. Standing, I stretch my limbs. "I think I'll take a quick shower. I stink."

My sister wrinkles her nose in agreement.

"Don't protect my feelings or anything."

Her laughter follows me down the hall to the bathroom.

I'm standing in the dormitory hallway toweling off my wet hair after a quick shower when Starling bursts out of his room, his own hair wet and sticking up in all directions. He quickly pushes it down, probably in an attempt to look respectable.

"Where are you going?" I ask, noting his eager expression.

He freezes in the middle of the hallway, easing around to face me. "Nowhere."

I chew the inside of my cheek.

He hides it well, but Starling is lying to me.

"Carry on," I say.

The boy gives me a grateful smile before practically running in the opposite direction.

Clarity pokes her head out of our room. "What was that about?" she asks, her shower caddy in her hand.

I peer down the hall toward the den, but see nothing. "I don't know, but I'm going to find out." With my hands on her shoulders, I push my sister back into our room and close the door behind us, locking it in place. Swiping my ear bud off my desk, I turn it on and pop it into my still damp ear. It's just a hunch, but I'm guessing Royal and Darnay called Starling into the control room. For what reason, I don't know.

"What are you doing?" Clarity asks, peering at me, arms crossed.

"Shh," I hiss, lifting my finger to my lips. "I need to hear this."

Royal's voice comes over the earbud.

Perfect. He hasn't found the bug I placed under the conference table. Yet.

"I'll leave you to it," he says. "Good luck."

"Thanks, old friend," Darnay responds.

A door closes, probably the one to Royal's office.

Someone clears their throat.

"Ah, there you are," Darnay says over the comms, his voice eager.

"Here I am." It's Starling.

My muscles tense. What the hell is going on?

"Now that you've been here for a few months, I wanted to… see how you're settling in." Darnay's words are slow, uncertain.

My instincts hum. Why would he be talking to Starling like that? Didn't they just meet, right after Starling arrived at the Tower?

Someone exhales. "It's going well, I think. Everyone here appreciates me, unlike at the Academy."

Fingers tap on the conference table's plastic surface. "Yes, I heard you had trouble with some of the other cadets."

"And yet you never came to visit." Starling's voice is angrier now, accusatory.

My mind is reeling. Why would Darnay ever go to visit Starling at his former school? Unless...

"I didn't want to make it worse for you."

Starling scoffs. "Of course not. I'm certain the reason you never came to Blackpool Academy was because you were thinking of me, your only son."

My heart stops. "No." The word escapes before I can stop it.

Clarity's eyebrows shoot up in question.

I spin away from her, my mouth hanging open. I can't believe it. It can't be. He would have told me.

Disappointment and anger rise in my chest, fighting for dominance, until they're a swirl of hot emotion in my head, clouding my thoughts. My fists curl into tight knots as I try to remain calm.

"What's going on?" Clarity asks in her usual serene but penetrating manner. She must sense my anger, because she circles around to face me, leaning down to catch my gaze.

A loud sniff shoots from my nostrils. "Nothing."

Her eyebrows rise even higher, but she holds her tongue.

"In a minute," I plead, waving a hand in the air. "Just, give me a minute."

"All right." My sister doesn't move from her position at my front, waiting.

Giving myself a mental shake, I focus on what I'm hearing.

"It's true," Darnay says, his voice less assured. "I didn't want to make a commotion at your school. I thought staying away was better for you. Truly, I did."

An angry snort in response. "You think not seeing my father more than once a year is better for me?" The edge in Starling's voice slices through the air.

"I've been to see you three times since you came here!" The older man sounds flustered as he tries to reason with Starling. His flesh and blood.

His only son.

My pulse pounds in my ears.

"I've been wondering about that. Why the sudden interest?" A pause. "Or is there something else going on?"

"No, no. I just want to make sure you're doing well here. Working for Royal could be very beneficial for you." The way he emphasizes the word "beneficial" makes my skin crawl.

Starling must agree with my assessment, because he sighs in frustration. "Please, leave. I'm just beginning to feel that I fit here, and I don't want you mucking it up. No more unannounced visits."

It's silent for a moment. What I wouldn't give to have eyes in the control room right now.

When Darnay speaks, it's with resignation. His words are cold as he says, "As you wish."

Fabric rustles. Probably Darnay's expensive suit.

"Father?" Starling asks, barely above a whisper.

"Yes?" There's a hint of hope in Darnay's voice.

My heart slams against my ribs.

Whatever Starling was about to say, he must think better of it. "Never mind."

The line goes silent.

Still I wait. Five seconds. Ten.

The low vibration of the concrete exterior door opening and closing courses under my feet.

Darnay has exited the Ivory Tower.

And I'm left in a swirl of confusion and distrust.

My sister must see the slackening of my concentration. "Loveday, what's going on?" she asks, putting a hand on my upper arm.

My teeth clench. My instincts war within me, fighting between spilling everything I just heard to my sister, or locking it up tight.

But Clarity is nothing if not persistent. "Hey," she says, shaking me. "You promised not to keep secrets from me anymore, remember?"

I do remember. It was a pledge extracted on our flight home from Sicily, after I had told Clarity all about the glimpses I'd been having of my dead mother. Glimpses that turned out to be my Aunt Megan toying with me.

"Here, have a seat." Clarity pulls me down onto her bed, a mattress on the floor, its blankets and sheets balled up at its foot.

I pull my knees up and wrap my arms around them, hoping the position will allow me to keep the anger coiled in my chest. Anger I can deal with. It's the other, more delicate emotions that I try to avoid. Exhaling slowly, I speak. "Starling is Charles Darnay's only son."

"What?" Clarity's mouth falls open. "Do you think Dad knew about it?"

"Of course he knew," I spit, realizing that I'm just as angry at him as I am at Starling.

"The question is, why didn't they tell us? They must have had a reason." Clarity leans back on her hands, letting her head fall. Always the trusting daughter.

23

"It doesn't matter."

My sister lifts her head, eyeing me. "Of course it does."

I bite my tongue, not willing to argue with her. But she's wrong.

Chapter 3

I pace across our room, running my fingers through my hair. My first instinct is to march into the control room and throw down with Starling, all furious missiles firing. But I can't follow my instincts in this. Royal trusts Starling, so I should, right? Doubt niggles at the back of my mind. There are things Royal hasn't told us in the past, things that I should have been informed of, but is that the case here? I gnaw on the inside of my lip. The last thing I need is to make a scene, not right after I've been reinstated to our team. It's been an exhilarating six weeks, and I don't want to lose that.

Yet, the cold truth is that the person I thought I was getting to know, beginning to care for, has been lying to me for months.

And so was Royal. Again.

My fingers drag down my face as I spin toward my sister. "What should I do?"

Clarity sighs. "Talk to Starling. I'm sure there's a reason he didn't tell you."

I cock my head at her. "Why are you always right?"

She grins. "Someone has to be."

I snort. "Indeed."

My instincts are screaming at me to stay away from Starling; avoid getting into a fight. But I can't evade him during the team meeting Royal has called. My skin prickles with annoyance as I step into the control room. The only seat remaining at the long conference table is right next to Starling. I sink into the chair and sit with legs crossed, so I'm facing away from him.

I may understand why Royal didn't tell me about Starling's parentage, but the boy could have at least hinted in that direction and let me figure it out.

A muscle in Starling's jaw tightens.

Royal strides out of his office and stands at the end of the table, at Julep's shoulder. "We've gotten a new assignment, from the CIA's chief operating officer, Gillian Harris."

Julep's eyebrows shoot up as she swivels to face him. "My old boss?"

"The very same."

"What does she want us to do?" Julep asks, yanking on one of her black curls.

"One of her IT guys, Ray Parks, is in the wind. She wants us to find him."

"No problem. Has Haru looked into his financials?"

"Already done," she chirps from one of the desks near the front of the room. Planting her feet on the floor, she spins her chair around to face the rest of us.

Royal nods. "He hasn't purchased anything in the past two days, and I mean anything."

"So either he's using cash, or someone else's face," Lotus says. He contorts his features into a silly expression, making Clarity smile.

Another nod. "It looks that way. She wants us to swing by his house first and poke around. Hopefully we'll get a bead on his whereabouts."

26

I purse my lips, mulling it over. "He's from their IT department?"

"That's correct."

"What were his responsibilities, exactly?"

"I'll give you one guess," Royal says, putting his hands in his pockets.

There are a lot of possibilities, but I doubt the guy was your basic computer maintenance worker. Gillian Harris wouldn't come to us for someone with low clearance like that. No, it has to be something that would worry her enough to come to us instead of sending the local police. I snap my fingers. "Cyber security."

"Bingo."

"Does that mean he was responsible for keeping their information offline?" Starling asks. "Preventing the leak of classified documents?"

"That's exactly what it means," I say, irritation in my voice.

Royal levels his gaze at me, his face inscrutable.

I make my face go blank, hoping I'm not in for a lecture. I'm really not in the mood.

His eyes skim over each member of my team, weighing our strengths. "Loveday and Starling will take point. Julep and Lotus will provide backup, if necessary."

My eyebrows shoot up. "Shouldn't Julep come with me, since she actually worked in the CIA office?"

My dad shakes his head. "Her specialty is undercover work, not covert assault operations. Although she's proven capable at both."

Julep gives a derisive laugh. "Thanks?"

I open my mouth to protest further, but Royal holds up a hand. "Is there a reason this assignment is distasteful to you?" His eyes bore into me, making me want to creep out of the room.

Instead I remain firm, arms at my sides, maintaining what I hope is an aura of ease. "No. It's not a problem."

"Good."

Across the table, Clarity relaxes in her chair, and pulls out a book. Is she relieved to not be participating in today's job?

Royal interrupts my line of thought. "Get your gear and get moving."

I nod, and then spin on my heel and march down the hall to the armory. I'll worry about Clarity later.

Starling is right behind me.

I enter the long, narrow room and stand in front of my gun safe. Using my palm print, I unlock it and swing open the heavy door. I'm eyeing my weapons when Starling's head appears over the top of the safe door.

He folds his arms along the top rim of the metal and rests his chin on his hands. His expression is open, unguarded. "Would you like to tell me why you're practically snarling?"

"No."

Starling's eyes widen at the sharp edge in my voice. "When will be a good time—?"

"Later, once we're not on the comms anymore."

He rears up, clearly confused by my change in demeanor toward him. "Have I—?"

"Later," I bark, refusing to look at him. Instead, I busy myself with loading my gun and stowing extra ammo, along with my knives, into my utility belt under my trench coat.

Starling hovers in my periphery, watching me make my preparations for our job. His mouth opens to speak, but after a beat he clamps it shut and turns toward his own gun safe.

We gather the rest of our equipment in silence.

Chapter 4

The drive from the Ivory Tower to our target's home is rife with tension, but as we draw closer to our destination, it eases. It's as if both Starling and I have decided to put our personal drama on hold while we're in the field, without having to talk about it first. I take a deep breath in relief.

Starling points at a house up the street on the right. "There it is."

I pull to the curb in front of Ray Parks's house. It's a small, boxy Federal-style home with a gray brick facade and white trim. The grass in the yard is a little long, and whatever plant was hanging in the basket on the porch is dry and shriveled.

A grimy, white sedan sits in the driveway. The license plate number matches the registration we found in Parks's name.

"When was the last time he used his vehicle?" I ask.

Haru answers over our earbuds. "The GPS hasn't moved from that spot in three days, since he got home from work on Monday night. Same with his phone."

I chew on the inside of my lip. "And Harris didn't say anything about him acting strangely at work that day?"

"No, his co-workers said he acted the same as usual.

Polite, focused, drank lots of coffee."

"All right." I cut the engine and unbuckle, but make no move to exit the vehicle. "What else do we know about this guy?"

"He's thirty-four, single, no family in the area," Starling puts in, his voice devoid of emotion.

"And a huge amount of debt from online poker playing," Haru adds.

"How much was it again?" Lotus asks over the earbuds.

"Twenty-one thousand dollars," Starling says.

I tap my fingers on my thigh. "That's a whole lot of losing hands."

Julep's low, long whistle pierces the heavy silence.

The blinds in the front windows are open, and there's no movement inside. No lights on either. "Does she think he's in financial trouble? Is that the working theory as to why he's not showing up for work?" I ask.

"She doesn't know, but any time one of her employees disappears…"

"It's a red flag, sure," I say. "Especially when they work in cyber security."

From the passenger seat, Starling shifts his upper body to look at me. His right arm stretches along the window sill. His dark eyes are focused on the task at hand. "How do you want to do this?"

I look past him to the house. "You said you couldn't find any indication of a home security system in his records, right Haru?"

"That's right. For a cyber security guy, he hasn't purchased any subscriptions, cameras, sensors, or anything."

"Hmm." I unlock my door, slide out of the car, and stride through the unkempt grass.

Behind me, Starling does the same. "So? What's our move?"

I glance over my shoulder up and down the street. There aren't any cars close by. "We pop into the backyard and see if Mr. Parks has a hide-a-key."

Starling's eyebrows furrow. "People still use those?"

"We'll see." I approach the side gate, which is standing ajar. Slowing, I pull my weapon out of its waist holster and motion for Starling to do the same.

Conveying my intentions with a hand gesture, I step aside as Starling approaches the gate. With a quick shove, he pushes it open. The coast appears clear.

I creep into the backyard, my eyes scanning for potential threats.

The space behind the house is even more unkempt than the front. The grass is longer here, and weeds sprout out of the ground at random. The concrete slab patio is cracked in a Z shape, and the rain gutters are overflowing with dead leaves from the oak tree that towers over the south side of the yard.

A dusty patio table and four chairs sits near the back door, as does a trio of terra cotta pots whose occupants are black and withered.

"It's safe to say he didn't have a green thumb," I whisper.

We edge along the back of the house, keeping below the window line, and check the side yard on the north side. It's empty.

Creeping upward, I peek into the house, but there's no movement within. I catch Starling's eye and motion toward the back door.

He nods in agreement.

"We're going inside," I whisper.

"We're here if you need us," Lotus says. He and Julep are

31

waiting in his car, which is parked a couple houses down from our location.

I cross the patio and, on a hunch, lift each of the dirt-filled flower pots. No key. I guess I have to give Ray Parks a little credit. Stepping up to the sliding glass door, I peer inside. It's locked, and there's an old broom pole in the doorframe. Even if I picked the lock, I wouldn't be able to slide it open from the outside.

The interior of the house looks cluttered, but orderly.

"There aren't any signs of a struggle," Starling whispers.

"Let's get inside." Taking my laser glass cutter out of my utility belt, I get to work.

Starling stands back, keeping an eye out for movement in the yard.

The faint buzz of the laser is the only noise as I cut a hole big enough to crawl through. Once I'm done, I ease the glass pane out of its place and prop it against one of the patio chairs. "Cover me," I say to Starling, and then I hunker down to shimmy through the opening. It's a tight squeeze, but I make it. Standing up, I hold my gun at the ready, scanning the small dining room, kitchen, and living room without making a sound or taking a step.

The air is stale, but it doesn't smell like anyone has died in here, so that's promising.

I remove the broom pole from its place and unlock the sliding door as quietly as I can.

Starling steps into the house and closes the slider behind him.

With guns raised, we sweep the house.

"There's no one here," I say once we've finished. "His toothpaste, toothbrush, and laptop are gone. I'm assuming he took some clothes, too."

"It looks like he was in a bit of a hurry," Starling adds. "Since his drawers were left hanging open."

"And there's been no financial activity?" I ask, my eyes falling on the cell phone that sits on the wooden surface of the desk shoved under the window in the master bedroom. It's still plugged in to its charger. There's a wide open space where I'm guessing his laptop used to be. The scuffs and stains along the surface hint at the many hours he spent sitting here, hunched over his laptop, gambling his money away.

"Not a cent," Haru says. "It's as if he up and vanished."

"Not many people can do that without leaving traces of evidence behind," I mutter, scanning the room.

My mind focuses on the details. "Let's talk this through. The guy works for the CIA. He spends his days defending confidential government information from would-be hackers and information terrorists. Then, he goes home to an empty house, eats a microwave dinner, if the overflowing garbage can in the kitchen is any indication. Then he, what? Spends his evenings gambling on his laptop? So what would make someone like that go on the run?"

"Maybe he owes money to the wrong sort of people," Starling says.

"It's either that, or something to do with work… There haven't been any security breaches at the CIA in the last two days, have there?"

"Nothing reported," Haru chirps. "It's business as usual over there."

Starling strokes his chin with long fingers, making a mock thinking face.

My mouth twitches upward, and Starling breaks into a happy grin.

An idea sparks. "Where is the closest hotel? One that

might still accept cash?"

Starling's gaze meets mine, a questioning look in his eyes.

"If I wanted to hide, I wouldn't go to a fancy hotel. I'd go to a dumpy one. You know, the kind that rent by the hour? Where they don't ask questions?"

My partner's eyebrows rise, and he grimaces. "How unsavory."

Haru's fingers click over her keyboard. "There's one about half a mile away, on Mars Avenue."

I nod to Starling. "Let's go check it out."

He follows me out of the house. "Do you think he'll be there?"

We climb into our car and buckle our seat belts. "He hasn't used the facial payment software in three days, and he didn't take his car or his phone, so he didn't want to be tracked. I'm guessing he walked somewhere he could hide. The question is, why?"

It takes us three minutes to find the hotel.

The Pair A Dice is one of those crusty drive-up motels with a couple RVs and a handful of minivans in the parking lot.

I pull my trench coat on and belt it closed to hide my gear.

On the other side of the car, Starling dons a perfectly tailored, navy pea coat that not only hides his holster, it accentuates his square shoulders.

We stroll into the rental office and sidle up to the counter. To one side, there's a clear plastic stand stuffed with travel brochures. See the Capitol! one says. Another promises a comprehensive list of all the haunted buildings in the area. A third uses clever wording to describe a tasting tour of the district's most upscale restaurants.

A middle-aged man with thinning brown hair, pasty skin, and a snaggle-toothed smile steps out of the back room, eyeing us. "Can I help you?" he asks, clearly annoyed at being interrupted by two teenagers.

"We're looking for my uncle?" I ask, putting on a pleading, wide eyed look. "We're close, and I haven't heard from him in a couple of days. Sometimes he comes here to clear his head. I just thought…"

"We don't give out rental information," the man huffs. He starts to turn away from us, but I reach out to grab his arm.

"Please," I beg, tears forming in my eyes. "My uncle, he's diabetic, and sometimes he forgets to take his insulin. It could kill him, and he's all I have left." My lower lip trembles, and I swipe at the tears building behind my eyes.

"Help us out, will you?" Starling asks. "Please?"

The man behind the desk perks up upon hearing Starling's accent. "You're English?" he asks. "I've always wanted to go."

Starling smiles. "It's a beautiful country."

The man's eyes flick to me, and then back to Starling.

"If I help you out, do you think you can give me some tips on when to go? What to see?"

Starling gives an easy smile. "It'll be my pleasure."

The instant the manager opens the hotel room door, the putrid stench of death hits our nostrils. He jumps back, clutching at his throat and gagging.

"Oh, that's bad," I say pinching my nose with two fingers.

Starling does the same, his face contorted in revulsion.

"I think we found Ray Parks," I say into the comms, "but I don't think he's in a position to answer questions."

"Come again?" Royal asks over the earbuds.

"Give me a minute to confirm." I take a deep breath of fresh air and step inside the room. None of the lamps are on, and the blinds are shut tight. With light fingers, I move to push the bathroom door open. It swings inward with a bang.

Ray Parks's body is crumpled in the bathtub, a length of bright orange cord strung over the curtain rod and fastened to the door knob. The other end is tight around his neck.

Chapter 5

Starling, Clarity, and I sit around the conference table in the control room, not speaking.

Starling's skin is still tinged with green from the sight of a man's body lying broken in that motel bathtub. The cup of hot tea Julep made him is clutched between his palms.

I'm guessing I don't look much better. My fingers grip the water bottle Clarity set in front of me, but the roiling in my stomach prevents me from trying to drink it. The last thing I want is to lose my breakfast in front of most of my crew.

Closing my eyes, I push away the images. Bluish skin. Contorted limbs. The orange cord, pulled taut. My mouth goes dry. I uncap the bottle and take a tiny sip, clutching the plastic lid in my other hand. My stomach leaps at this, but I manage to get it under control.

Beside me, Starling stirs in his chair and runs his hands down his face. "What now?"

At the head of the table, Royal stands with his arms crossed. "Are you two all right? Tell me if you'd like to talk to someone."

Starling nods stiffly. "Thanks."

Royal's eyes turn to me, and mine fall to the floor. "I will."

In my peripheral vision, I can see him watching me. He must be satisfied with what he sees, because he continues the meeting. "The CIA will investigate Mr. Parks's death, but right now it looks like a suicide." His jaw ticks, drawing my eyes to his neck.

An orange cord hovers over my vision. I bolt out of my seat. "I need some air."

Clarity stands, eyes wide. She reaches out and grabs my hand. "Why don't we walk to the drug store? I need to pick up a couple things anyway."

I give her fingers a squeeze. "Sounds like a plan."

"Good." She scoops up her molasses-brown leather clutch and hugs it to her.

I pull her out of the control room toward our room. "Let me just change first."

"Are you guys going somewhere?" Haru is peeking at us from the open slit of her bedroom door, a curious smile on her face.

Clarity returns the gesture. "We're going to the drug store. Please come."

"Great! Just give me a sec." Haru ducks into her room, closing it behind her. There's a rustling noise from inside, and then she opens it just wide enough to slither through the narrow opening.

My eyes register curiosity of my own.

She pulls her bright yellow hoodie on over her ivory button-up shirt, but not before I catch sight of long, red scratches on her forearms.

"How did you get those scratches on your arms?"

Haru's eyes go wide. "I, um…" She casts around for something to say. Finally, she looks at me with a tight smile. "You know those vases in the lobby with the fake, twisty branches? I knocked one over, and the sticks scratched me. Clumsy, huh?" She pulls her slick black hair up into a hasty ponytail. Her eyes skitter along the wall toward the ceiling as she pulls it tight.

"Yeah, clumsy." I don't believe a word of it.

It seems that Starling isn't the only one lying to me.

I tamp down the frustration I'm feeling, determined to enjoy this outing. We don't get out of the Ivory Tower nearly enough, aside from when we're working. Maybe some fresh air and sunshine are exactly what I need.

Clarity, who is standing in between us, hooks her arm through my elbow before doing likewise to Haru. "Here we go," she says.

I scan the den, my eyes skimming over the slouchy couch and chairs, the scuffed wooden coffee table, and the glowing sconces. Farther in, the metal door separating the den from the entry is firmly closed. There's no sign of Starling.

We're almost there. Hopefully we'll get outside without coming across the boy. I really don't feel like talking to him right now.

Something in the den creaks as we cross its shabby carpet.

Clarity tenses, her steps slowing.

My instincts are on high alert.

Something isn't right here.

I turn to check behind us.

"Boo!" Lotus jumps out of the kitchen stairwell, arms raised.

Clarity, Haru, and I jump a foot into the air and land laughing.

The tension in me is broken, and I can't stop the giggles that come pouring out.

Lotus grins. "Gotcha." He pokes Haru in the side, sending

us into further peals of laughter.

"You are so dead," I choke between breaths.

"Uh huh, we'll see," Lotus says as he struts around us. "I got you ladies *good*."

"Oh, it is on," I retort.

Holding his hands wide, he shrugs. "Come at me."

Raising my chin, I smirk. "Sleep with one eye open, brother."

"How many times have I told you—?"

I don't wait for his mock tirade about how we are not siblings. "Later!" I pull Clarity and Haru along behind me as I barrel along the service tunnel and out into the parking garage.

Behind me, Haru is still trying to contain her giggles. She stoops low, swiping at her face.

"Are you crying?" I ask, eyes wide.

"I can't help it," she says. "I was laughing so hard! I almost peed my pants."

Clarity smiles. "That was fun." She turns to me. "How are you gonna get him back?"

I scan the parking lot, my eyes catching on Lotus's car and motorcycle, parked neatly in the shade of the hulking cement structure. "I'll find a way."

Clarity's smile widens. "Count me in."

It's a flicker of the old, more serene Clarity that I haven't seen since we've been home from Sicily, and the sight of her lifts a weight off me. Maybe she's going to be okay after all.

Lotus, on the other hand…

I push the thought aside, wishing to save plotting for later. "So, Haru, how are your folks?"

She pales, her smile fading away.

Clarity smacks me upside the head. "You have no subtlety at all!"

Rubbing at my smarting scalp, I apologize.

"It's okay," Haru whispers, sending me a fleeting smile.

"It's just, I know she misses her dad." I shrug. "I was trying to be supportive."

Clarity shakes her head. "Lead with that next time."

It's my turn to cook dinner, so I'm in the kitchen making pizza dough, just like Rosa, our host during our time in Sicily, taught me. I've found that using my hands in this way is highly satisfying, watching the flour, salt, yeast, and water come together into a meal that will be delicious when it's ready. Plus, it helps set the stage for my first prank on Lotus.

"It'll be ready in twenty minutes," I call up the stairs to my teammates, all of whom are engaging in a session of mock-the-action-movie in the den. Loud laughter is all I get in response.

Rolling my eyes in amusement, I return to the task at hand.

I'm so focused on working the dough that I don't hear Starling coming down the stairs until he's right beside me, moving in to kiss my cheek.

I jump back, startled.

"Whoa," he says, laughing. "It looks like you're wound pretty tight. Let me help." He steps behind me and puts his hands on my shoulders in a light touch. "Tell me if this is too hard." His fingers press into my skin.

"No. Don't." I roll my shoulders and pull away from him. "I'm busy."

His mouth curves upward. "Too busy for a shoulder rub?"

"Since you're the one offering, yes." My earlier anger at his dishonesty flares in my eyes.

Starling frowns, takes a step toward me. "What's wrong?"

"Not now." I shake my head, digging my fingers into the

dough and refusing to look at him. I don't want my pizza dinner to be ruined, which is exactly what will happen if I get into this conversation with Starling right now.

"What is it?" he presses.

"Seriously. Not. Now." I punctuate each word by slamming the pizza dough down on the floured counter top, sending a white cloud of dust into the air.

He coughs. "All right, I'll leave you alone. But promise me we'll talk later. Okay?"

"Fine." Still, I won't look at him.

Starling slumps and moves to take a seat at the table. Taking out his phone, he peers at it.

Every furtive glance in my direction irks me even more.

I work in silence, channeling my anger into kneading the dough, before separating it into two large balls. In a few minutes, I've got two gorgeous pizzas: one with all of my favorite meaty toppings, and one vegetarian, for Haru.

Opening the scorching oven, I slide them inside and shut the door.

Then, I set about pouring drinks. Each of my teammates gets a cup filled to the brim with ice cold, bubbling soda.

Except for Lotus.

Starling eyes my movements, the corner of his mouth tilting up. "What are you doing?"

What I want is to ignore him, but Royal's voice filters through my head. Drilling manners into my skull. "You'll see," I respond coolly. Once I'm finished, I set the table, putting each person's cup in front of their usual spot.

The timer on the oven beeps, signaling that the pizzas are done.

Peering inside, I glory in the heavenly smell and the bubbling cheese. I make quick work of slicing the pizzas with a rolling cutter.

Starling gets plates out of the cabinet and sets them on the counter. "It looks delectable," he whispers.

"Thanks." Satisfied with my work, I trek halfway up the stairs. "Come and get it!"

Lotus, Haru, Clarity, and Julep come galloping into the kitchen, hovering over the pizzas and scooping the piping hot slices onto their plates.

I hang back, watching as Lotus sits in the seat I knew he would take, and brings the cup of brown liquid to his lips.

Anticipation courses through me. Sweet revenge.

He takes a big gulp and his eyes go wide. He splutters, gagging on the disgusting drink I concocted for him.

Julep's eyes screw up in concern, but Clarity, realizing what's going on, starts laughing. She whispers to Haru, who does the same.

Cautiously, Starling starts laughing too.

Puzzled, Julep turns to me. "What's going on?" She pushes down her own urge to join in, though I wish she would. Her loud, brassy honk of a laugh always brings a grin to my face.

"Gotcha," I yell at Lotus, firing finger guns at my still-coughing victim.

He wags his tongue, his features contorted in a grimace. "What is this?" he finally pushes out, eyes squeezed shut.

"Carbonated water, barbeque sauce, chili powder, pureed sweet relish, mustard…"

Lotus mimes gagging. "I've heard enough. That was pretty sneaky."

I curtsey, grinning like the Cheshire cat. "Thank you."

He wags a finger at me, eyes glinting. "You're going to regret this."

"That's unlikely," I shoot back. "But give it your best shot."

"Count on it." Lotus takes a photo of the pizza, which looks delicious if I do say so, and pockets the phone.

"Why are you taking photos of your food?" Haru asks, taking a bite of the vegetarian pizza.

Julep hides a smirk behind her hand.

Lotus's gaze cuts toward me. "I, uh, started a foodie feed on My Life Now. You know, to share all the amazing stuff I get to eat. I didn't think it'd be a problem."

My eyes widen. "You know you can't show any of our faces, our location, anything on there."

His lips purse. "Come on, give me some credit. All it is is my hands, plus all the mouth-watering food. And nobody is there for my hands."

Julep lets out a snort.

"See?"

Sighing, I relent. "All right. But you have to be meticulous. And you can never post a location, restaurant name, city, anything."

He cuts across me with a casual head bob. "I gotcha. Don't worry. For now, let's eat this killer pizza."

Chapter 6

I focus on my image in my watch screen, making sure I don't have pizza sauce smeared on my cheeks. Baring my teeth, I inspect them for bits of food. Once I'm satisfied, I knock on the door to Royal's office.

"Come in."

I slide the door open and step inside, closing it behind me. Nerves coil in my shoulders, adding tension to my already tightly-wound frame.

"Loveday. What can I do for you?"

I lick my lips. I'm already pretty sure what he'll say. It's the same reason I'm supposed to pretend I don't know Lotus is from Chicago, or that Haru uses her real name. Still, I have to ask. "I just wanted to ask you something." I sink into the chair opposite his airplane-wing desk, running my finger over the battered and scuffed metal surface.

Royal leans to one side, resting his chin on his knuckles. "Go ahead."

I shift in my chair, leaning forward with my forearms slung over my knees. Stalling. Royal always has reasons for keeping information from us. I don't always agree with him, but I need to remember that he does it to protect us. I take a deep breath.

My dad's eyebrow rises. He eyes me, waiting.

I scan the wall of bookshelves behind Royal. The souvenirs from a hundred trips abroad. The framed handgun hanging in a glass case. The row of Ian Fleming novels he reads when he gets bored, which, admittedly, is not often.

"Loveday."

I force my gaze to Royal.

"You said you had a question for me, so ask it."

Steeling myself, I do. "Why didn't you tell me Starling was Darnay's son?"

His eyes rise to the ceiling, and then fall to meet mine. "We've discussed this. At length."

"No, we haven't."

A muscle in his jaw twitches. "I don't allow you and the rest of your teammates to share personal information, for your safety, and for that of your family members. The less you know about their lives outside the Tower, the better."

I frown. It's not a good enough answer. "But it's Charles Darnay we're talking about. He can handle himself." I can't hide the disdain in my voice.

Royal leans forward in his chair, locking his gaze on me. "Do you really think you would have been so *accepting* of Starling if you'd known who his father was?"

My gut clenches. It's generous of him to call my early attitude toward Starling "accepting" at all. It's not the word I would have chosen. Grudging. Openly hostile, maybe. Not generous. My tongue feels sluggish in my mouth. I don't want to own it. "You're right," I push out finally. "I wouldn't have." Guilt swirls in my chest. If I had known Starling was Darnay's son, I would have been unmerciful. Since Darnay wasn't around after Vale's death, Starling would have felt the brunt of my wrath.

Royal's laptop beeps as a notification comes in. His eyes slide down to it before returning to me. "I'm going to consider this matter closed. Let's not speak of this again."

"Agreed."

"Call everyone to the control room, will you?"

Royal stands at the head of our conference table, arms folded casually over his chest. "COO Harris has another request for us."

"Not it," Lotus says.

When Royal turns his heavy gaze on the boy, Lotus's shoulders rise to his ears. "What? I don't wanna be the next one to find a dead body." He shivers. "Gross."

Pursing his lips, Royal faces the rest of us. "On that indelicate note. The higher-ups at the CIA are concerned about the security of their information. Mr. Parks's death, when taken into account with Nexus's attempt to acquire the files in Charles Darnay's possession, and The Chin's absconding with the facial recognition software the CIA uses for on-sight security, is troubling. They're concerned he'll try an attack on CIA headquarters directly."

My entire body goes still, and my brain jumps to red alert. "They think he's after the non-official cover list."

Royal nods. "Exactly."

"The NOC list is real?" Haru asks. "Really? I thought that was just something they made up for the movies."

Starling shakes his head. "MI6 has one as well. At least, that's what I've heard." He shoots a look at me.

"They do," Royal says with a glance in his direction. "It's how they keep track of their agents in deep cover around the world."

"How detailed is this list?" I ask, leaning forward in my chair.

"If Nexus gets his hands on this list, every CIA agent in the world will be compromised, or worse. The CIA would have to pull every single one of them, and I can't stress how catastrophic that would be."

"Whoa," Lotus says, itching his nose.

"Indeed."

"What does all this have to do with us?" I ask, gesturing to my teammates.

Royal's eyes gleam. "They want to know if Nexus could use the facial recognition software to break into CIA headquarters in order to retrieve those files."

Haru taps her fingers over her lips. "It would be tricky. He'd have to hack into their security and change one of their employee's profiles to match his own face, sneak into the building, get around their internal safeguards, and into their server room. I'm guessing those types of files can't be accessed remotely. Then there's the matter of getting the data off the premises."

Lotus's eyes go wide. "Damn. I thought I was the only one obsessed with those old Mission: Impossible movies."

Haru grins. "My dad is a huge fan of Tom Cruise."

"Old school," Starling says with a smile.

"Now that that's settled," Royal says, leveling a serious look at Lotus. "Let's focus, please."

Lotus ducks his head, wiping the silly look off his face with one hand.

Under the table, Starling taps my shoe with his boot.

I scoot farther away, still refusing to look at him.

He leans toward my ear, lips parted, but I don't give him the chance to speak.

"What does this have to do with us, exactly?" I ask, popping the collar of my coat and pulling it tighter around me. "Try to break in and steal the files ourselves?"

"Now who's obsessed with Tom Cruise," Lotus taunts.

But Royal smiles, his blue eyes alight. "Exactly."

Chapter 7

Excitement ripples through me. We're actually being asked to break into the CIA, for real? "Can you repeat that?" I ask, wanting to make sure I heard Royal correctly.

"The COO of the CIA has asked us to perpetrate a covert assault on their headquarters with the objective of sneaking into their server room and downloading their complete list of agent files onto an external device, which we will then smuggle out of the building. Is that clear?"

"Hell yeah," I say, pumping my fist.

Lotus holds his hand out for a high five, and I oblige. "Yes," he exclaims.

"This is going to be interesting," Starling says, shooting a surreptitious glance my way.

Julep agrees, tapping her pointer finger on the table top. "Here's what you need to know."

Royal puts a hand on her shoulder to stay her words.

They exchange a look.

Her expression smooths over and she sits back in her chair.

"You were saying?" Lotus prompts.

"I can't tell you," Julep says.

My brows bunch together. "Wait. Why can't you help us? You've been there, unlike the rest of us. And so has Royal, for that matter."

Royal leans over the table, resting his weight on his fingertips. "The COO wants us to go in blind, just like Nexus would do, so Julep and I can't help you. I've arranged for Clarity to attend a tour of the CIA's headquarters with a student group on Tuesday. She'll observe the layout, security, and any other important details, and report back to us."

At this, Clarity tenses in her chair, her brown eyes round. "You want me to go in? Shouldn't Loveday or Starling go instead?" She spaces out the words, as if she's trying to appear casual.

Royal shakes his head. "Loveday and Starling will go in on the day of our attempt, and we can't risk anyone recognizing them. And since you're our resident disguise expert, I thought you'd enjoy the opportunity to put your skills to use."

Clarity swallows and nods quickly. "Sure, it sounds fun."

But her nervous tone belies her words.

"Are you sure, Dad?" I ask. "I'm sure we could put together some type of disguise for me."

My sister shoots me a grateful smile.

"Clarity goes," Royal says, his tone firm. "You and Starling will provide backup from a vehicle stationed far enough away so as not to be suspicious. This is a training exercise. No one will be hurt. Any questions?"

Six heads shake in the negative.

"Good. Now get some sleep. It's late, and we have a lot of work to do."

As one, my team stands and moves toward the hallway.

Royal catches Starling's arm and says something low in his ear.

Starling nods, and then turns to leave.

"Loveday."

I halt at Royal's resigned tone, and turn to face him. "Yes?"

He holds a hand out to me, palm open.

On it is a tiny listening device.

My skin prickles and my eyes fly up to his face. I'm busted.

"Do not bug the control room again."

Schooling my face to remain blank, I take the bug in my fingers. "No, sir."

Royal turns and goes into his office, shutting the door behind him.

But when I swivel around to leave the control room, my heart lurches.

Starling is still standing in the doorway, his eyes locked on the listening device in my hand.

My eyes go wide. "It's not what it looks like," I say in a rush.

His jaw clenches as he stares at the bug in my palm. With effort, he wrenches his eyes upward to meet mine. "You heard what Royal and Mr. Darnay discussed a few days ago." The light of recognition dawns in his eyes. "This is why you've been avoiding me for the past few days."

I nod.

"You were spying on them, on *me*." The accusation in his tone rankles me. He wasn't honest about who he is, so I had every right to find out by other means.

My chin lifts. "So what if I was? Darnay lied to us, and one of our own was killed. You think I'm going to sit around while he ropes us into another mission without giving us all the facts? No way."

He breathes out through his nose, his smoldering eyes still

locked on mine. "You had no right to eavesdrop on us."

My eyes narrow. "How else am I supposed to know if you're lying to me about, oh I don't know, your parents?"

His hands ball into fists.

I've struck a nerve.

"Darnay is your dad?" I ask, incredulous. "And you didn't think I'd want to know?"

"I never lied to you," he says, his voice low as he fights to calm down. He takes a step toward me. "Don't you trust me?" The words burn as they spew from his lips.

I should take a breath, try to calm down, but instead I barrel ahead. "How am I supposed to trust you?" I shoot back. "I barely know you!" My statement rings through the air, hitting Starling like a punch to the gut.

But every word is true.

We hardly know each other.

His deep brown eyes fall to the floor, his mouth drawn into a tight line. "Then what are we doing?" he asks, the words a mere murmur.

I wring my hands. "I don't know." Raking my fingers through my hair gives me a moment to consider. The past few weeks have been amazing, and I don't want to lose that. But on the other hand, there is so much I don't know about Starling, and the truth about his dad is only the start of it. What if there's more he's hiding?

Seconds pass in silence.

Starling's eyes search for mine. He takes another step forward, reaching for me. His lips part as if to speak.

I don't let him. "Whatever this is, it's over."

And with that, I push past him toward the dormitory, running to get away from the hurt I've just inflicted on Starling, and on myself.

Chapter 8

Clarity is standing outside our door with the latest edition of her favorite glossy fashion magazine in her hand. She rips out whole pages carelessly and uses sticky goo to mount them to the wall, adding to her ever-growing collage of makeup and clothing inspiration that frames our doorway. The edges of the collection creep toward Julep's room on one side, and the bathrooms on the other, slowly covering every inch of the wall in glittery, photo-shopped images of women in flashy clothing and disco-ball makeup.

"What do you think?" she asks when I approach.

My head bobs. "It looks good, very glamorous."

"Oh, hush," she says, batting at me with the brick of a magazine in her hand.

"Watch out," I say, laughing as I evade her attack. "You could kill me with that thing."

"You know what they say," Clarity smirks. "Beauty is pain."

I force a chuckle at this.

Haru's door opens a crack, and she peers out. "What's going on out here?"

A whiff of a scent I can't identify emanates from her

room.

I step forward, sniffing the air with curiosity.

Haru's eyes widen. She slips out and shuts the door behind her, cheeks pink.

"What have you got in there?" I ask. "What's that smell?"

Next to me, Clarity stills, both hands prepared to rip another page out of her magazine. She wants to hear Haru's answer, too.

Haru's blush deepens, and she shakes her head. "Nothing. I just… I spilled a bottle of perfume. It smells a little funky in there now."

"Right."

She's lying again, although I can't imagine what she'd have to hide. I already know about *her* parents. Her eyes skip up and down the hallway, making sure no one else is in earshot.

Starling is nowhere to be seen.

Lotus's and Julep's doors are open, but they're not home. They left for a run a half hour ago, so they won't be back anytime soon.

"What's up?" I ask.

"I'm having trouble focusing in class. I think Ms. Truly noticed. She caught me drawing anime characters in my notebook when I was supposed to be taking notes."

"That's not great," I prompt.

"No," Haru says, but she doesn't sound convinced. "I'd just rather be here."

I shrug. "Royal promised your mom you'd get a good education, right?"

She nods eagerly.

"So, that's what he's trying to do. And really, you could have it much worse. Truly is easy. Just… try to pay attention when she's talking, and you'll be fine."

"Okay, I will."

The screech of paper being torn asunder fills the hallway as Haru skitters into her room, careful not to let me get a glimpse inside.

"She's definitely hiding something," I breathe, looking at my sister.

"Aren't we all?" is Clarity's only response.

Chapter 9

My fingers drum on the steering wheel as I maneuver Royal's beat-up Civic through the pouring rain. The car's windshield wipers beat at the water pelting the glass, hoping to make headway, but it's as futile as trying to block an ocean wave with nothing more than two frantic hands.

A chill runs through me.

I'm not one hundred percent sure this is what I want.

I haven't seen my Aunt Megan since the U.S. consulate worker in Palermo came to take her away. Now, she's in prison here in the states on kidnapping charges.

Charges she received for helping Beppe Arnoni kidnap my sister right out from under our noses, back in St. Petersburg.

There's no way she'll be found not guilty, not with the evidence we brought back from Sicily. Not with Clarity's testimony.

You'd think I'd never want to lay eyes on her again. Never hear her voice. Never see her smug satisfaction at making Royal pay for his supposed sins.

But you'd be wrong.

This woman, my aunt, has two decades of memories with her sister, my mother, that I can't access any other way. It's not like I have any other family to ask for stories about my mom.

So I drive on through the rain, hoping that the squirming my stomach is doing, that the taste of bile in my throat, will dissipate once I reach my destination: Baltimore Women's Correctional Facility.

It took some work to convince Royal this was a good idea, or at least not a terrible one.

After repeated attempts on my part to persuade him of how badly I needed to hear stories about my mom, he caved.

With gritted teeth he called a friend in corrections, who greenlit my visit. The guy even made it so I could get into the facility using a false identity. Can't afford to leave a trace of myself on a government facility visitor list, can I?

I exit the freeway just south of Baltimore and weave the car through the rain-slicked streets, the GPS giving me directions when necessary.

Years ago, Clarity and I programmed it to have teen heartthrob Chris Lake's voice, and it still does.

"Turn left," Chris croons, drawing forth a smile.

"Never gets old," I whisper.

Chris says that I've arrived at my destination.

My alert eyes fix on the building to my right, and I pull into the parking lot.

The three story, cement block of a building would look grim in the fairest sunlight, but in the chilling wet of today's thunder storm, it looks downright sinister.

Rain has soaked the top third of the building, coating it in a dark stain that drips along its roofline and creeps down toward the regularly spaced slits in the cement that represent windows. A person could barely fit an arm through such a narrow opening, and I'm guessing they don't let in much light, either.

I pull into an empty parking space facing the building and shut off the car. My heart is racing but I can't force myself to pry my fingers off the steering wheel. They refuse to budge, instead clinging to the wheel's worn rubber coating, making my knuckles go white.

Rain batters the car, mimicking the slamming motion my heart is making against my ribs.

Now that I'm here, mere yards away from where my aunt is being held, dare I go in?

She accepted my application to visit, so I'm pretty confident she'll agree to see me, but something holds me back.

Will it really help to listen to Aunt Megan talk about my mom? Will it make the woman I've daydreamed about all my life feel more real to me?

Or will it paint in my mind the image of a woman who is no closer to me than the moon?

I stare at the building, waiting for a sense of peace to come and settle my warring insides, but it doesn't.

A man gets out of a car nearby and opens the back door. Leaning in, he unstraps a small boy and carries him across the parking lot. The boy's eyes meet mine only for a moment before he cranes his neck to look at the ominous building his ahead.

I lick my lips. I can do this. It's just my aunt. She can't hurt me in there. She won't look anything like my mother in such a controlled environment.

Still, my hands won't relinquish their grip the wheel.

I can't do this today.

Reaching down, I start the car's engine, back out of the space, and speed away through the rain, my heart still pounding in my chest.

Each stroke of Clarity's makeup brush has me mesmerized. The colors swirl on her skin in grays, browns, and reds, her face becoming a canvas of rotting, bleeding flesh.

"You're going to make one freaky zombie for Halloween," I say from my desk chair, where I'm sitting reading my mom's old volume of Grimm's fairy tales. Since I chickened out of talking to my aunt, it's the closest I can get to my mom, for now.

"Mmhm," she replies, mouth open for balance as she applies a swipe of black liner around her eyes. Then she turns to me. "How do I look?"

"Like an extra on that old zombie show."

"Perfect." She stands and takes the few steps to her dresser, rummaging through it, for what, I don't know. "Where is it?" she mumbles to herself. "Aha!" She straightens, holding one of Vale's old metal band T-shirts.

I inhale at the familiar tightening in my chest.

Clarity glances at me, and freezes. She must be reading the pained expression on my face. "Is it okay if I use this for my costume? If not, I can put it away…" Her voice trails off as she meets my eyes.

"No, it's fine. Use the shirt. He'd love it."

My sister smiles, making her zombie makeup look even more garish.

"Quit it," I say. "You're creeping me out."

Tossing her hair, Clarity plops into the desk at her vanity, takes out a pair of cuticle scissors, and starts cutting holes in the shirt at random.

I wince at the first one, choosing to focus instead on my book.

A trill of raps on our door interrupts me, making me swivel my head in that direction.

"Let me answer it," Clarity whispers with a grin.

A tilt of my head toward the door signals my agreement.

With a deft twist of her wrist, Clarity flings the door open and yells, "Boo!"

Haru screeches, jumping back and cowering in the hallway.

Laughter bursts from me as I stand. "Well, that worked."

"Oh no!" Clarity exclaims, hunching over Haru, patting her shoulder. "I'm so sorry."

Haru peeks up at her between shaking fingers. "Why, why do you look like that?"

"Practice for Halloween."

Haru gulps and pushes herself to stand. "Can I come in for a minute?"

"Be our guest." Clarity waves her over the threshold into our room.

Beyond them, I note Haru's bedroom door is shut tight.

"What's up?" I ask once all three of us are safely ensconced in our room with the door closed.

Haru fidgets in the middle of the floor, pulling the neon yellow sleeves of her hoodie down over her hands. "I think I'm in trouble with Truly."

I give her a skeptical look. "What could you possibly have done to make Truly mad at you? The woman's basically a saint."

"And don't think she hasn't tried to rile her," Clarity adds, jutting her thumb toward me.

I shrug. "True."

Haru shakes her head. "I'm doing my best, but I guess it's not good enough. She, she asked Royal to come talk to her this evening. It has to be about me, right?"

I steeple my fingers. "You haven't put a cockroach or a big moth in her desk, have you?"

Haru's wide eyes fly up to mine. "What? No! I would never. Eww." She shivers in disgust.

Clarity snickers.

"Truly feels exactly the same," I say, smirking.

"You mean you, you...?"

"Put various creepy crawlies in her desk? Yeah, I did."

"You should have heard Truly scream," Clarity puts in, smothering her smile under her hand.

"That's terrible," Haru exclaims, shaking her head. "I would never do that. My parents would say I'd disgraced them." Her faces blanches.

"Harsh."

Clarity's head bobs in agreement.

Haru sits listlessly on my sister's desk chair, her arms curled around her knees.

"All right," I say, rubbing at my hair. "You are her only student right now." I draw out the words, thinking them over. "How's it been going when you're up there? Are you focused, working hard?"

"Well..." Haru's eyes drift over the floor. Then they jerk to mine. "I have to do well here, or Royal will send me back to my parents. My father will be so disappointed in me. And my mother..." She covers her eyes in her hands as if to block out this possibility.

"It sounds like you simply need to try to pay attention in class. If you do that, everything should be fine."

"And maybe apologize to Truly," Clarity puts in. "I love her." A sigh escapes as she leans past Haru and examines herself in her vanity mirror. "More gangrene, I think." She swivels her head to hover within inches of Haru's. "In the meantime, want to be a zombie?"

"Um, no thanks," Haru says, her color slowly returning.

"I'd better go do some homework."

"You do that."

The girl turns to go.

"And Haru?"

She looks over her shoulder at me, a question in her eyes.

"You're going to be fine. If I can't get on Truly's bad side, you have nothing to worry about."

Hope shines in her expression as she leaves our room, tiptoeing into her own and shutting it tight behind her.

I look after her, studying her closed door. "What do you think she's doing in there?" I mutter.

Clarity sits at her desk, adding mossy green eyeshadow to an angry red wound on her forehead. "No idea, but it's probably harmless."

Chapter 10

The streets around the high school where we're dropping Clarity are crawling with people. Teenagers pile out of cars on both sides of the road, slinging their backpacks over their shoulders and giving their parents half a glance goodbye before fading into the throng streaming up the stone steps into the school building.

The students who are lucky enough to drive pull their cars into the long line that threads into the parking lot, waiting their turn and hoping they'll get a parking spot.

A car pulls away from the curb and I swoop in to take its place, garnering several honks from frustrated drivers who were eying the same stretch of asphalt. Too bad for them.

In the passenger seat, Clarity is quiet, her eyes flicking over the crush of people. There's a small device in her hand, about the size of a pack of gum. "I hope this thing works," she says, gripping the item with long fingers.

"It'll work. As long as you're in a room for more than ten seconds, it'll be able to scan its measurements and mark any points of ingress and egress. Just try to visit as many rooms as possible."

My sister's voice is barely a whisper. "I will."

I reach over and put a hand on her thigh.

She turns to look at me, her expression solemn.

"We'll be right outside the building. If you need us, we'll get inside, no matter what."

My sister gives me a tight smile.

Starling leans forward, sticking his head between our seats. "You can do this, no problem."

I fight the urge to push him away.

"Thanks," Clarity says, her smile lifting. "You're right. I can do this."

"Easy peasy," I say, though my voice is nowhere close to light.

Starling turns a serious look at me. "Easy peasy?"

Jutting out my elbow, I tap his shoulder. "Would you sit back please?"

"Yes, ma'am." He complies, his words clipped.

With a deep breath, Clarity rolls her shoulders back and opens the car door. "See you later."

"See you."

Then she's gone, disappeared into the pack of students heading toward the large yellow bus in the rear of the parking lot, near one of the school's side doors.

Starling gets out of the car and slides into the passenger seat beside me. "Ready to go?"

"Yep." I pull away from the sidewalk and navigate through town, trying to ignore the stifling awkwardness of being alone in a car with Starling, now that we're not dating, er, making out anymore.

"We're waiting to get on the bus," Clarity whispers, her voice coming through our earbuds loud and clear.

"You can do it!" Haru chimes in enthusiastically.

"Copy," I say, a hint of a smile on my lips. "We're on our

way to the park. Just keep your head down and you'll be fine."

"I will."

"This is so exciting," Haru continues. "My dad would flip if he heard I was helping you guys break into the CIA. I hope we get to use a helicopter."

I snort. "Choppers are too loud."

"And not very inconspicuous," Starling grumbles.

I glance at him, tilting my head in begrudging agreement. Haru gives a disappointed sniff, but doesn't say anymore.

My fingers drum on the steering wheel as we wait in traffic. It's the middle of rush hour, so a drive that should take us about fifteen minutes takes twice as long. Even so, we should arrive at CIA headquarters well before Clarity and the rest of the high school group do.

My eyes scan the area as we drive up George Washington Memorial Parkway toward CIA headquarters. I make the turn slowly, and approach the buildings. Pulling into an open space to the side of the lot near where the bus will be parked, I kill the engine and relax in my seat. "Here we are."

"Yes."

I unbuckle my seatbelt and pull my trench coat tight around me. The trees lining the property are still, their leaves unbothered by an absent wind. Still, it's not warm. I shiver, glad I wore my coat.

"We're loading onto the bus," Clarity whispers. "ETA forty minutes."

"Excellent," Haru says.

We fall silent, waiting to begin. Clarity's reconnaissance is our first step toward infiltrating the CIA, so we have to nail it. We won't get another chance to have eyes inside before we put our assault into motion.

"Haru, have you been able to get to the store? I'm craving

a blue energy drink." What I'm really asking is if she's been able to crack the CIA's digital storage. Clarity's foray into headquarters won't give us a complete blueprint of the building, which is what Haru's trying to find.

"I'm at the store, but it's crowded, so I'm having to step carefully. Don't want to run into anyone. I haven't found your drink yet."

Nodding, I look over the parking lot again.

No one has noticed Starling and I sitting in our car.

Good.

A few minutes pass in silence.

Several times I open my mouth to speak to Starling, but what would I say? My lips clamp shut, and I remain where I am, peering out the window, waiting for the school bus to arrive.

"We're five minutes out," Clarity says at last. "A couple of the kids may have seen me talking to myself."

"That's one way to perpetuate the myth that homeschooled kids are weirdos," I tease.

Starling turns to me, eyebrows raised in question.

I wave him off. "Not important," I mouth.

"I am not a weirdo," Clarity says, louder than she intends.

"Careful," I whisper. "Keep it down."

"Then don't bait me," she hisses. "I'm going silent. I don't want to draw any more attention. If I need you, I'll let you know."

"Roger."

"Good luck!" Haru exclaims, her voice flat in concentration. The tapping of fingers on a keyboard filters through my earbud. From the sound of it, Haru is typing *fast*.

After an awkward hour and a half, during which Starling and I both attempted to begin polite conversation with no success, we haven't heard from Clarity. Instead, the only voices we hear over the earbuds are the drone of the tour guide and the low chatter of the students around her.

I take that as a good sign.

Knowing my sister, she's keeping quiet so she can make note of the building's layout and security without drawing notice to herself.

I shift in my seat, kicking off my shoes and sitting cross-legged in the driver seat.

Starling is vigilant, one elbow resting on the windowsill, fingers wrapped around the handle on the ceiling of the cab. His eyes rove back and forth, watching as people and cars move around us. His thumb runs along the outer seam of his jeans in a slow motion that I'm pretty sure is unconsciously done.

I glance at my watch, marking the time.

"My favorite color is blue," Starling says in a low voice.

My head jerks up and I spin to meet his gaze. "What?"

His brown eyes are steady as he looks across at me. "You said you didn't know me, and I'd like to change that. My favorite color is blue. What's yours?"

My pulse picks up, just a tad.

"Isn't it obvious?" I ask, gesturing toward my outfit.

"Black."

"Yep."

"My favorite is bright yellow, like the buttercups back home!" Haru pipes in, sending cracks shooting through the awkward tension in the car.

Starling and I glance at each other. Amusement shines in his eyes, but he still doesn't smile.

My lips twitch.

"Favorite food?" I pose the question while scanning the lot beyond the windshield, fluffing up my hair.

"Scotch eggs. There's a pub near the Academy that fries them with sausage and bread crumbs, and oh, they're scrummy."

"That does sound good. I wonder if we could find them somewhere in DC."

"There's an idea," Starling says, nodding enthusiastically. "What's your favorite food?"

"Grilled cheese, or any of the crustaceans. Really, if someone were to give me a grilled cheese with shrimp or lobster, I'd die happy."

Starling makes a show of lifting his watch and typing a note. "Loves crustaceans. Noted."

"Oh! Mine is sukiyaki, it's like a vegetable and tofu stew," Haru says. "And pickles!"

A muffled giggle comes through the comms—Clarity.

"We'll try not to distract you anymore," I say, stifling a chuckle.

"Yes, my apologies," Starling adds.

Our sincerity draws a barely audible "Thanks," from my sister.

I sneak another look at Starling, who has resumed his surveillance of the parking lot, a smile draped across his features.

A flicker of pleasure warms my belly at the thought of Starling making an effort to deepen our friendship. Today is turning out to be not so painful after all.

Chapter 11

Haru's frenetic J-pop music is blasting down the dormitory hall when Clarity, Starling, and I enter the Ivory Tower.

My eyebrows rise. I'm surprised Royal would let her play it that loud.

I stride along the hall to the control room, but there's no one inside. That explains it.

"Where'd everyone go?" Clarity asks over my shoulder.

"Beats me."

"I'll put our gear away," Starling says, reaching out a hand, palm open.

Clarity and I remove our earbuds and hand them over.

"Thanks," we say together.

Starling inclines his head before moving off toward the armory.

I sling my arm around my sister's waist and pull her in for a side hug. "You did great today."

Her mouth lifts in a smile. "I think I got some specs we can use."

"Excellent."

Lotus's laughter wafts up the stairs from the kitchen, followed by Julep's loud, honking laugh.

"Let's go see what that's about, shall we?"

"Let's."

We tromp down the stairs and burst into the kitchen.

Lotus is at the counter, covered in flour. He's kneading a large ball of dough, creating clouds of white dust that rise and settle on his shoulders and in his curly black hair.

Across from him, Julep is hunched over her tablet, reading out instructions. Her cheeks are flushed from laughing, and her braids are spilling over her shoulders. Lotus's phone lays on the counter beside her, rimmed with floured fingerprints.

They both spin to look at us as we step into the concrete room.

"What's going on in here?" I ask, crossing the room to peer at Julep's tablet.

Julep's eyes twinkle as she speaks. "Rosa sent us the recipe for her focaccia, and Lotus wanted to try it. As you can see, it's—"

"It's going fine," Lotus says, cutting her off. "Pretty soon we'll have hot, crusty bread to eat. And I'll have a good looking photo for my foodie account."

"Mmhm," I back away, trying to avoid getting covered in flour.

"I can't wait to try it," Clarity says, her tone lighter than it's been all day. She settles at the long wooden dining table, pulling her book out of her bag and sticking her nose in.

Julep's eyes glide to Clarity's face. "Is it done?" she asks, the corner of her mouth twitching.

Clarity's expression twists in disgust, and a shiver rolls through her body. "Yuck. Yes, it's done."

"Excellent," Julep responds, chuckling. "They're in for quite a surprise."

"Indeed," I say. "Where'd Royal go?"

"He went up to check in with Truly," she says, pushing her braids behind her shoulders.

"Again?"

Julep shrugs.

Without looking up from the bread dough under his palms, Lotus asks, "What do I do next?"

Julep focuses on her tablet, running her finger over the screen. "Let it rest for ten minutes."

I take the opportunity to duck up the stairs, striding through the den and into the dormitory.

My knuckles make a loud rap on Haru's door.

Within, the music gets quieter. "Sorry about that," she yells without opening the door. "I turned it down."

I wait a beat to see if she'll answer the door.

She doesn't.

A sigh escapes my lips. "Do you know why Royal went upstairs to talk to Truly again?"

Haru squeaks. "He did?" Her voice is higher pitched now. "Yep."

"I have no idea. I hope I'm not in trouble. I'm trying to focus more, do my best on my homework…"

She's winding herself up, her words coming quicker.

"I'm sure it's fine," I say. "Don't worry about it."

When she speaks, it's a single word, uttered under her breath. "Okay."

"Have you found the blueprints for CIA headquarters yet?"

Her answer is smaller still. "No."

"Keep at it."

"I will. Ow!"

"Are you okay?" I ask, bending closer to the door to listen.

"I'm fine. I'll let you know when I find something."

I could swear I hear a jingle in Haru's room, but what would make a sound like that?

"Thanks." I go into Clarity's and my room and pull open my desk drawer to complete my post-mission ritual. Pressing my finger to my lips, I lean down and pull out two shiny frames.

But I'm not greeted by photos of my mom and Vale.

No, instead my eyes land on grainy, poorly printed color photos of Nicolas Cage, eyeing me with a wild expression.

"What the ...? Lotus!"

I groan as the watch on my wrist vibrates, waking me up. It's pitch dark in our room. The scent of Clarity's lavender moisturizer permeates the air, as does her shallow, unconscious breathing.

I withdraw my arm from under my squashed pillow and squint at the screen, pushing a button to illuminate the message I've received.

Royal
Meeting at 07:30.

It's nearly 07:00, so I don't have time to go back to sleep. With another, louder groan, I slide off the side of my lofted bed and land with a thump on the carpet. Crossing the room, I kneel and pat Clarity's hip where she's sprawled out on her mattress on the floor, the covers kicked off the end of her bed in a wad.

She flinches awake, pushing her sleeping mask up her forehead and blinking her eyes to focus on me. "What is it?" she asks, sitting up. Her brunette hair stands out in wavy points around her head. A cavernous yawn escapes her. "It's early."

"Royal's called a meeting in half an hour."

She nods, scratching her side with long, delicate fingers.

I scoop up my bathroom caddy and meander down the hall toward the bathroom.

The doors to Royal's Starling's, and Haru's rooms are shut tight, but Lotus's door is ajar.

Just as I pass it, a short, female giggle emanates from inside.

I freeze, not sure I believe what I just heard. Is Julep in there with Lotus? At 07:00 in the morning? I shove the thought away, not wanting to think about the implications. Thinking about Lotus in any sort of romantic capacity activates my gag reflex, especially after that fantastically gross kiss we shared in Palermo. A shudder runs through me.

Not wanting to get caught standing outside Lotus's door, I make for the bathrooms.

That's when Julep decides to stroll out of his room, adjusting her black camisole top as she comes.

Our eyes lock and she halts in place, a sheepish smile on her face.

"I was just…" she trails off, probably deciding that no matter what she says right now, I already know what she was doing in Lotus's room in the middle of the night.

I hold up my free hand. "It's none of my business." I start to move past her, but she stops me with a light hand on the crook of my arm.

I twist around to meet her gaze, a questioning look in my own.

"It won't affect our performance," she says. "I swear it."

"I can't exactly lecture you about that," I say with a smirk. "With my history."

Her smile relaxes. "You're doing just fine, boss."

A low chuckle escapes me. "Thanks. Carry on." I lock the bathroom door tight behind me, glad that I have the place to myself.

Royal would be angry if he knew Lotus and Julep were… involved.

And what if he found out that Starling and I were doing whatever we were doing?

I'd end up with a smaller squad, that's for sure.

Some people would end up shipped off to Siberia, I'm just not exactly sure who.

Chapter 12

Another surprise awaits when I walk into the control room. There's a breakfast spread on the conference table. I'm talking pastries, fresh fruit, bagels, smoked salmon, and various flavors of cream cheese.

"Whoever thought of this, I'm a fan," I say, sinking into a chair. I swipe an everything bagel and pile it high with chive and onion cream cheese, finishing with paper-thin slices of smoked salmon.

"Whoa, remind me not to sit next to you this morning," Lotus quips, pulling out the farthest seat away from me while waving his hand in front of his nose.

"You know you love me," I say, sending a great big, stinky breath his way.

Lotus pretends to gag, eyes squeezed shut. Sliding to the ground, he holds his throat and coughs. "Toxic gas. Must escape…"

Clarity's laugh tinkles from the doorway. "What's going on in here?" She takes one look at my plate and her eyes go wide. "That looks delicious. Thanks!" She sits in the chair next to mind and serves herself a raspberry danish and a pile of the freshly cut fruit.

"It wasn't my idea," I say.

"Truly suggested I feed you guys breakfast, instead of making you eat cold cereal or toaster pastries," Royal says as he comes out of his office, closing the door behind him.

My eyes pop. It's been quite a while since I've seen our former teacher. "Truly suggested this? Remind me to thank her the next time I see her."

The corners of my dad's eyes crinkle. "I'll tell her you appreciated it when I see her this afternoon."

"You're having a conference with her about me, again?" Haru asks in a shaky voice as she stands in the doorway with a tin of wet cat food in her hand.

Royal's gaze turns to hers, his blue eyes warm. "No, there's something else I need to discuss with Truly."

"What's the fancy tuna for?" I ask Haru, taking another big bite of my aromatic breakfast.

Her eyes widen in question, and then she realizes I've spotted the can gripped in her fingers. "Oh this? There's a cat that's been hanging around the hotel parking garage. I've been feeding it."

"If you feed it, it'll never go away," Julep says as she strolls into the room, looking sharp in one of her brightly-colored skirt suits. She sure gussies up quickly. "Good thing I love kitties," she finishes. She sits beside Lotus and dishes a large serving of fruit onto her plate.

Haru blushes. "Me too! I've always wanted one, but my mom…" The color drains from her face. "She doesn't like animals, so I was never allowed to have a pet."

"My aunt loves animals," Starling says as he enters the room. "Oh, breakfast." He plops down in the chair beside me and loads up a plate with a bagel, danish, and some of the fruit. He turns to me with a smile. "Good morning."

"Good morning," I say, my mouth turning up in a wicked grin when his nostrils flare at my abhorrent breath.

Lotus cackles. "See? That's why I'm sitting way over here."

Starling laughs. "Indeed."

"Thanks for breakfast, Royal," Julep says after swallowing a bite.

"You're all very welcome," he responds. "But it was Truly's idea."

Julep's eyebrows rise in surprise, but she pulls them down. "Good idea," is all she says.

We eat in silence for several minutes, the only sounds in the room the scraping of plastic silverware on thick paper plates.

Once we're about done, Royal wipes his mouth on a napkin, and speaks. "This is just a quick reminder as you finalize your plans for breaking into CIA headquarters. Our job is to spot any holes in their security, and advise them how to plug them. Their security detail will be armed with tranquilizer guns during the exercise, as will all of you. Everyone is to operate under the rule of doing no permanent harm to any member of the opposing team. It should be an exciting, and illuminating, experience. You're tasked with something that no other group of spies has been sanctioned to do, so use the opportunity wisely." He eyes me as he says this. "Some of you may wish to work for the CIA proper in the future, and this would be a great time to impress them."

I smile, looking at Clarity.

Her return smile is wide, but there's something else behind her eyes I can't quite pinpoint.

"Does everyone understand?" Royal asks, his hands loose in the pockets of his camel-colored slacks.

He's met with a chorus of, "Yes, sirs."

"Then I'll leave you to your planning." He excuses himself with a nod.

Once he's gone, Haru leans forward, her eyes shining. "I've got something I think you're going to like. It'll make this a lot more interesting." She shifts her weight to one side and pulls a miniscule thumb drive out of the front pocket of her bright yellow jeans. "It looks like a thumb drive, but it doesn't have storage space. Instead, it's got an app on it that displays a fake download progress bar and a countdown when you plug it in to a computer. It'll simulate actually stealing the CIA's NOC list and agent files so you know approximately how long it would take to do it for real. What do you think?"

Lotus crows. "Sweet. That'll put a fire under her, for sure."

"Bring it on," I say, holding out a hand for the drive.

Later, when we're alone in our room, Clarity gives me a mischievous smile. "I think Dad likes Truly."

"What?" I say, eyes wide. "No way."

"Think about it. He's suddenly going to meetings with her, letting her convince him to order us a fancy breakfast…"

I shake my head in disbelief. "I think you're reading too much into it." There's no way Royal would date Truly. They've been friends for years. Just friends.

The women's prison doesn't look so bad in the sunshine. The high midday light cuts shadows into the sidewalk around the side of the concrete edifice, but the run-of-the-mill cars in neat rows over the parking lot make the place look almost like a commercial building. Almost.

It's the coin-slot windows that give away the structure's true purpose.

I flip down the visor and check my wig. It's an ashy

blonde, shoulder length lob with lighter blond highlights. If I grew my hair out, this is pretty much what it would look like. Every hair is in place, so I slip out of the car, locking it behind me.

My tennis shoes scuff on the pavement as I step onto the sidewalk, my pace slowing.

My stomach clenches. It's one thing to think about visiting my aunt Megan, visualize what it would be like to have an actual conversation with her about my mother, without Royal or Julep or Starling hovering over me. But going through with it…

I shake off the doubt. I can do this. With a deep breath, I pull open the ballistic glass door and step inside.

A shiver runs through me, raising goosebumps on my arms. It's freezing in here. I run my hands along my bare skin, wishing I'd worn my trench coat, even though the sight of a teenager in such a getup would probably have raised alarms among the prison's security personnel.

Instead, I'm wearing dark wash jeans and a heather gray tee shirt. Basic. Normal. Unremarkable.

The woman at the front desk, who is wearing a faded denim prison staff uniform, looks at me with a blank expression. Her name tag reads Brandy. "Reason for visit?" she drones, blinking in slow motion.

I step up to the counter and retrieve my fake driver license. "I'm here to visit my aunt, Megan Sanderson, please?"

"Fill out these forms. The prisoner will be notified that you are here, and may or may not agree to see you. Bring these back when you're done." She hands over a clipboard with a black ink pen chained to it. "Front and back."

I nod, taking the proffered item and sitting in one of the worn, plush and wood chairs lining the small waiting area.

Brandy picks up her phone and speaks into it, letting the person on the other end of the line know that prisoner Megan Sanderson has a visitor.

My pulse quickens as I try to force my nerves to calm. I push my gaze down to the clipboard clutched in my hands, and fill out the forms. It doesn't take long before I'm back at the counter, handing the paperwork over to Brandy.

She types something into her tablet and holds it over the forms, scanning them into her device. "The prisoner will see you. Step through the door, please."

A buzz sounds, alerting me that the door leading further into the building is unlocked.

I push it open and find myself in a narrow hallway.

Two prison guards block my path, one male and one female.

The woman steps forward. "Lift your arms."

I comply, and she pats me down, thoroughly but gently. "Clear."

After asking me a series of mostly benign questions, she waves me down the hall, where I step through another door.

Inside, the large room looks like a cafeteria—fluorescent lights, round, veneered tables and plastic chairs. Two guards stand by the door I just came through, and two more guard a door at the other end of the room.

My heart thuds when I catch sight of my aunt sitting at a table near the back of the room, wearing an old orange jumpsuit, her hands visible on the table.

At my wrist, my watch vibrates.

It's a message from Lotus, but I ignore it.

Royal knows where I am today, and if anything came up he'd message me himself.

Taking even breaths, I walk across the room and take the

chair opposite my aunt.

She gives me a wan smile. "I was surprised to hear that you'd come to see me." Her voice is quiet, more timid. Her short time here has taken away her edge.

I shrug. "You're the only family I have left, besides my dad and my sister."

She shakes her head lightly. "That's not true. My parents, your grandparents, are still alive."

My jaw drops in shock.

It seems there's yet another secret Royal didn't tell me.

Chapter 13

It takes us all day and late into the night to plan our attack on the CIA. We're doing our best, despite not having completed blueprints of the building. Haru hasn't been able to get her hands on them yet. She wasn't kidding when she said it would be hard to access the CIA's secured files from an offsite computer.

By the time we've finished going through the plan several times and poking holes in it so we know our weak spots, we're all bleary eyed. Clarity's arm is splayed out over the table top and her head is a dead weight on her forearm.

"It's late," I groan pushing away from the conference table in the control room. "Let's get some sleep. Wheels up at 07:30." Anticipation bubbles up, making me shiver. Tomorrow is going to be intense.

"You got it," Lotus says, swiping at his droopy eyes.

Starling stretches his legs and pulls himself out of the chair, grunting in protest at having to get up.

Haru alone is still peppy. There's an actual hum of energy emanating off her skin, probably from the Japanese caffeine drinks her dad had shipped over at her request. "I'm not tired yet, so I think I'll take one more look for the blueprints." She quails at the commanding stare I aim at her. "Maybe not. See you all in the morning." She swipes up her laptop and scurries out of the room.

"Come on, you big lug." I pull on Clarity's arm to get her up from her chair.

"Carry me," she mumbles, leaning on me with all her weight.

"Ugh, I can't," I groan, listing to one side. "Too heavy." She laughs, but doesn't let go.

It's still dark when the Tower's security system gives the alert that someone's coming inside. But instead of the usual, low beep, an obnoxious pop song filters through the speakers. *"Take me to the dance floor, spin me around…"*

Clarity rolls over in bed, lifting her eye mask from one eye. "Is it time to get up?" she asks in sleepy voice.

I wipe my eyes with one hand. "No."

She pushes the mask up to her forehead. "Is this another prank?"

"You got it."

Her eyes widen. "What'd you do?"

"I programmed the security system to blast that dance pop song whenever Lotus comes into the Tower. It's the one that's constantly on the radio."

From the hallway, Lotus howls. "Argh! I hate Natasha Day. Make it stop."

I unlock my watch and check the security cameras. He's standing in the middle of the room, scowling, covering his ears with his hands.

Despite still having sleep in my eyes, I grin into the dark.

"But does it have to be so loud?" Clarity whines.

"Okay, I admit, it's louder than I thought it would be."

Down the hall, Royal's door opens. "What's going on?" His footsteps recede along the passage. There's a rushed conversation between the two of them.

A moment later, I hear it.

"Loveday!" My dad bellows my name, and someone stomps down the hall to bang on our door. "Shut it off, now!" he commands.

I bust up laughing at this. "Good thing I locked the door." Clarity snickers.

Lotus is out of the Tower by 07:30, taking his car to fulfill his part in the scheme. "See you in a few hours." He tips an imaginary hat at me as he leaves, his keyring spiraling around his finger.

Starling and Clarity are in the armory when I enter, already gearing up. They're so decked out that they look like members of a Special Forces unit. Starling gives me a lopsided smile. "This is more what I'm used to," he says, twisting from side to side to show off the gear he's got stowed at his waist, across his chest, and strapped to his back.

"I'm glad you're comfortable," Clarity retorts. "I can barely move in this stuff."

I pat my sister on the arm. "You'll be fine. Do your part. Make some noise, and I'll do mine."

Her doe eyes find mine. "Deal."

"You ready?" Starling asks her, his fingers reaching up to strap his helmet in place.

She does the same. "Yep."

"Then let's roll."

They brush past me down the hall, their heavy boots

sounding on the concrete floor.

"Hey," I call after them as I lean against the armory's door frame.

Both of them look at me, eyes expectant.

"Be careful. And have some fun, yeah?"

Starling smiles at this. "We'll do our best."

Then they're gone.

Royal and Haru meet me in the control room. My dad's gaze sweeps over me, taking in the creamy button-up shirt, houndstooth cardigan, black slacks, and sensible slip-ons. "If I didn't know any better, I'd say you look like an office worker. How many weapons have you got under those clothes?"

I smirk in response. "Enough."

"You look great," Haru puts in. "And Lotus is already almost to the rendezvous point."

"Great." I turn on the earbud in my ear. "I'm leaving now. I should be in place in half an hour. Then it's up to Starling and Clarity."

Haru's cheeks flush pink. "This is so exciting!"

"Yeah, it kind of is." I leave the Tower, my cross body bag bumping against my hip. My only thought as I slide into Royal's old car is, I hope Lotus doesn't have any trouble.

Despite the early hour, the CIA parking lot is already half full when I arrive. I park and extinguish the car's engine, my pulse already threatening to increase. Several deep breaths bring it under control. My eyes feel strange with the contacts in place, but I ignore the sensation. I haven't worn them in quite a while.

"Lotus, how are we on time?"

He fake coughs in response. *Right on track.*

I slide out of my car and march toward the entrance, head held high. I work here. I belong here. There's nothing to see. The glass door swings open under my hand, and I step into the lobby, my eyes dazzled by the clean, white lines of the large foyer. People walk through the security checkpoint, flashing their badges to gain entry to the stairs.

I swallow and approach the reception desk to my right.

"Good morning," the woman behind the desk says with a smile, but her fidgeting belies her confidence. She's nervous. "I'm sorry. I don't usually work the reception desk. Our regular receptionist is having some car trouble, so she's not here yet. What can I help you with?"

An easy smile rises to my lips. "I'm the new intern. I'm supposed to shadow COO Harris today?" My voice is low and timid, and I nervously brush a strand of my mousy brown wig behind my ear.

"That's right! I found a note about that in her calendar. Stephanie Garver, right?"

My smile widens. "That's me."

The receptionist hands me a visitor pass. "This will get you through security and up to Ms. Harris's office. Good luck!"

"Thank you so much!" I gush, before turning toward the bank of badge readers that blocks the way to the stairs. Here I go. The card reader turns from red to green under my visitor pass, and the electronic arm slides into the console, allowing me to walk through.

Any tension in my muscles drains away. This is going to be easy. I'll be in and out before anyone notices.

To hide my destination, I ascend the stairs to the second floor, and then double back down to the basement via the auxiliary stairs at the rear of the building. They're well lit, but not monitored by cameras.

That's a mistake.

My footfalls echo off the concrete. I've only got a few more steps to go before I reach the basement. Pausing, I glance upward. There doesn't appear to be anyone on the stairs above me, and the door to the basement remains firmly closed.

Creeping toward it, I peer through the glass pane into the room beyond.

There are eight desks in the room, divided by fiberglass cubicle walls. Due to the early hour, only two of the desks are occupied. It's not ideal, but it could be worse.

My fingers wrap around the door knob, twisting it so slowly it doesn't make a sound. My body trembles with nerves as I push open the door.

There's a low rumble outside the building, making my eyebrows shoot up. It's a helicopter.

And that's when a siren starts to wail.

Chapter 14

Both of the workers swivel in their desk chairs, staring at me with wide eyes. "What's going on?" the woman asks.

Adrenaline flows through my body as I step into the basement. I don't have much time. I put on a confused, frightened expression. "Please, can I stay in here until it's safe?"

"Who are you?" the man asks, standing. He pushes his glasses up his nose and eyes me. "You're not supposed to be down here."

"I'm sorry," I squeak. "There's a helicopter outside, and the siren is so loud. I came down here thinking it would be safer." My entire body trembles in fright.

His face twists in confusion. "A helicopter?" The man turns to the other worker. "Jojo, are we expecting anyone today?"

She shakes her head. "From the ear-splitting sound of that siren, I'm guessing not."

The man looks back at me, holding his hands out in a placating gesture. "You stay right here with my friend, Jojo, okay? You'll be safe."

I give him a nervous smile. "Thank you."

He moves past me and clutches the doorknob. The siren

blares as he pushes through the door and up the stairs.

I turn to Jojo, who looks nonplussed at being left alone with a frightened teenager. "Have a seat," she grumbles. "It'll be fine."

I hunker down in the still-warm chair the other employee was using. My eyes skitter toward a metal door to my left, where there's a palm pad and a facial scanner. "What does that lead to?" I ask.

"None of your business," Jojo says.

Despite the fact that I have no idea what's going on outside, I'm remarkably calm. Years of training have prepared me for this task.

Jojo returns her fingers to her keyboard, her eyes focused on her computer screen. And that's when I nail her in the shoulder with a tranquilizer dart. She slumps forward over her keyboard, her glasses falling off her face.

"You're heavier than you look," I grunt as I drag the unconscious woman over to the server room door. It's tricky, but I push her hand against the palm scanner. It beeps, and the facial scanner lights up. I manage to get her face in line with the panel by holding her under the armpits.

The light on the security panel turns from red to green, indicating that the door is unlocked. I scramble forward with one hand outstretched, pulling on the knob to open the door while trying not to drop Jojo.

Once I've got the door open, I drag her inside and prop her against the wall. The door locks with a satisfying click.

"I'm inside the server room," I whisper to Haru, even though I know Jojo can't hear me.

"Yay! Now get those pretend files."

"Roger." My eyes rove over the rows of computer towers in front of me. The other guy will be back any second, so I have to hurry. I take the thumb drive out of my pocket and stride toward the server banks, looking for a port to plug into. There! Peeling my mini tablet and aux cord out from the holster strapped to my waist under my blouse, I plug it into the server. Its screen lights up, ready.

I'm surprised when it allows me access to their hard drives without requiring a password. That's one hole in security they'll need to patch up once this exercise is over.

"Come on, come on," I say as I scan the thousands upon thousands of files. Finally! My eyes alight on the folders I'm looking for, but the heightened sound of the siren alerts me that the other computer tech has re-entered the basement.

"Jojo? Hello?"

A silent pause.

"Why is there a shoe…?"

My pulse leaps as I whirl to look at Jojo. Sure enough, one foot is encased in a flat black ballet shoe, but the other foot is bare.

Outside, the man pounds on the server room door. "Jojo? Are you in there?"

I jump at the sound, my eyes focused on the solid door.

"Jojo, are you in there? I just got an alert on my computer."

I don't move, don't make a sound.

"Are you okay? Why is your shoe out here?"

I don't even breathe.

"Intern? Are you in there?" The man's voice is less controlled as panic edges in. "Come out!" He shouts. "You can't hide in the server room. They've got the situation under control upstairs." His voice spirals higher.

My mind races. I could play terrified teenager again, but I doubt he'd buy it. One glance at sleepy Jojo over there with her one bare foot would give me away. No, it's better not to respond. Stick to the plan, Loveday. You're almost out of here.

"I'm getting security," he yells, panic giving way to anger.

My eyes lock on the mini tablet, watching the fake download-in-progress bar creep toward completion. I have to hand it to Haru; the graphics are slick. It looks just like a real progress bar. The tablet's graphics stall at 70 percent, and my heart slams into my chest. I don't have time for this. Hurry!

A minute passes in silence.

Sweat drips down my spine as I stare at the screen, willing the progress bar to move.

The download jumps to 80 percent, and then 90 percent. It's done! I rip the cord out of the port and shove everything back into the holster.

Footsteps pound down the stairs toward the basement.

Retrieving a screwdriver the length of my thumb out of the holster strapped to my ankle, I sprint across the room to one of the large air vents lining the wall. With all the computer servers in this room, it's important to keep them dry and at the ideal temperature, so the basement has its own, isolated HVAC system. Handy.

In a blink, I've got one of the vent cover's screws out of the wall.

The door to the stairwell eases open with a creak.

Above, the siren halts abruptly, leaving the air painfully quiet.

A whispered murmur of voices catches my ear.

I gulp, focused on the vent cover.

Footsteps approach outside the server door, and again someone pounds on it. "This is CIA security. Come out with your hands where we can see them."

I ignore them. The second screw comes loose.

I scramble for the third, willing it to come faster than the other three. No luck. It's stripped. I sit back on my heels, eyeing the next vent grate, but the sounds coming from outside the door indicate I don't have enough time to start over unscrewing the next vent cover. I shove my screwdriver into the head of the stripped screw, trying desperately to catch on one of the grooves.

Outside, the security panel beeps. They'll be inside in moments.

I've got it! The screw twists slowly, eking out of the wall in fits and starts.

Behind me, the door flies open.

The screw falls out and I twist the vent cover away from the opening, its metal frame scraping against the wall. I'm halfway into the air duct when behind me I hear weapons cock.

A man's voice comes, firm and emotionless. "Freeze right there."

My blood runs cold.

I've been caught.

Officers Murphy and Campbell crow about their victory as they usher me into the lobby. "You should have seen your face! You were so scared," one of them teases me. "Nice try, distracting us by having your friend fly through unauthorized airspace in a chopper."

Embarrassment flames up my neck, forcing me to lower my eyes. Although I know that it's a good thing I was stopped by CIA security from completing my mission, it still doesn't feel good. My lips purse. Our plan was bold, and it should have paid off, but it didn't. I'm no closer to plugging the holes in the CIA's security than I was a few hours ago.

"Your commanding officer is coming to pick you up. You can wait at reception. Right over there."

I pull my arm from Campbell's grasp. "I know where it is." My low heels click over the tile floor as I make my way to the desk.

The regular receptionist, Maureen smiles up at me from her usual place. "I heard you tricked my replacement this morning," she drawls with a smile. "Very impressive."

"Thanks." A flicker of pride glows in my chest. She knows I tricked her sub, but she doesn't know I had Lotus puncture her car tire so she'd have a flat, and then pose as a rideshare driver to ferry her all over creation instead of bringing her straight to work.

Maureen gestures toward the lone chair by the information desk. "Have a seat."

I take the chair she indicates and slump my head against the wall. At first, it rankled that I had failed in my objective, but now the part that bothers me most is that they've seen my face. Even if I ditched the wig and contacts, they might recognize me next time.

My fingers drum on my thigh as I wait for Royal to come pick me up. I had the chance of a lifetime—to do something no other spy has ever managed to do—and I blew it. Spectacularly. So much for impressing the higher-ups in the CIA. I may have just failed not only at my mission, but at my greatest chance at a future in intelligence.

Chapter 15

I start bargaining as soon as I slide into the car. "You have to get us another shot. We can do this."

Royal's gaze shifts to mine as he reverses and pulls onto the street. "I'll talk to Gillian, but I can't make any promises. We only discussed one attempt. And they'll have plenty of data to work with after your near-win this morning."

"But I didn't complete the mission. I'm sure there's another way to get those files, and it's only a matter of time before someone finds it. Wouldn't you rather that person was me?" Instead of Nexus. I don't have to voice the words; we're both thinking them.

Royal clears his throat. "Like I said, I'll talk to Gillian."

I nod, taking that as final. It's out of my hands for now.

Starling and Clarity are waiting for us when we enter the Tower. "How'd you rope that pilot into flying over CIA headquarters?" Starling asks. He's changed out of his gear into olive green cargo pants and a gray tee. "He wouldn't tell us."

"He owed me one."

Clarity tilts her head, probably wondering how I got leverage on an air force pilot. "Let me guess, classified?"

"You know how it is."

"Of course."

"If you'll excuse me, I have some work to do." Royal pats my shoulder before disappearing into his office and closing the door behind him.

Starling moves toward me. "Let me help you stow your gear."

I start to protest that I can do it on my own, but something stops me. "Thanks."

My sister's eyes flit between us. "See you in a bit." She wafts away toward the dormitory.

Starling leads me into the armory and waits while I unlock my gun safe.

"Turn around." I say, pausing until he's facing away from me to lift my shirt and unstrap the holster from around my abdomen. The velcro gives with a loud screech, and I can't stop the sigh of relief that escapes me. "I don't know how Julep wears these all the time. They're hot and itchy."

Starling chuckles. "Is it safe to turn around?"

"Go ahead." I tuck the gun and ammo into their proper places in my safe, and then close the heavy door with a satisfying thunk.

"I'm famished. Let's go see if we can find something to eat."

"Ready for afternoon tea?"

"Hey, don't mock afternoon tea. It's delicious, and the perfect way to bridge the gap between lunch and dinner on the days when you're feeling famished by 16:00."

My expression grows sober. "I thought I had them. The files."

Starling stops where he's standing in the doorway. Turning, his gaze finds mine. "It was a brilliant plan, but plans don't always work the way we expect them to." His eyes lower

97

as if he's speaking from experience.

"I know, but it still bothers me. I've never failed to accomplish an objective before. There have been close calls, sure, but I've always gotten the job done. This thing, today, it's a first. And I have to be honest: it doesn't feel great."

"I can sympathize. My father…" His jaw clenches. "He pushed me hard. He expected perfection, and when I didn't meet his standards…" Starling's eyes darken.

My heartstrings tug at this admission. "I'm sorry. I didn't know. I thought he was… gone all the time?"

"It didn't stop him from writing emails to express his disappointment."

"Emails? Classy."

Starling huffs.

"I guess I'm lucky. Royal doesn't make us feel bad when we don't perform the way he expects. He tells us what we need to correct, and you saw how he benched me a few months ago, but deep down I know he'll always support Clarity and me, no matter what."

A wan smile crosses Starling's mouth. "You have no idea how lucky you are."

"I'm beginning to."

A comfortable quiet falls between us as we reach the den. "Are you still hungry?"

Starling looks down at me, a pleased shine in his eyes. "Definitely."

"I found a great English pub nearby. They make those scotch eggs you like. Want to go?"

"Absolutely."

It's nice to have someone I can talk to openly, who seems to get me. And from the look Starling's giving me, it looks like he feels the same way.

Chapter 16

Despite the in-depth conversation our entire team had about how to improve on our first attempt on the CIA, Royal hasn't breathed a word about Harris letting us make a second one. And for some reason, we don't have another job lined up at the moment. My weather app says it's a nice day out, so I leave the Tower, an idea blossoming in my mind.

It's a clear, almost warm Saturday for fall in D.C. I stroll down the sidewalk, enjoying the sun on my skin. The brownstones lining the street glow a copper color in the bright afternoon. The scent of aging leaves permeates the air, drawing my eyes to the colorful canopies of the trees lining the sidewalk.

Near the end of the block, I stop. My eyes travel up the facade of the three-story brownstone in front of me, from the terra cotta pots edging the stairs, to the gleaming brass house number, to the crisp curtains hanging in the windows.

Truly's house.

I haven't been here in a couple years, since I graduated from high school.

As I climb the steps, I'm reminded of all the time Clarity and I spent here as kids. Truly was always our teacher, from

99

kindergarten up through high school. From the alphabet to multiplication to chemistry, she was our guide. We met her home three times a week, along with the kids of several other CIA employees for classes, projects, and experiments.

Of course, once my family moved into the Ivory Tower, Truly met us privately in one of the hotel's conference rooms, but those bare spaces don't hold the memories of this singular brownstone.

I scale the steps and announce myself using the dainty brass knocker. Turning over my shoulder, I check to make sure I wasn't followed, but there isn't anyone suspicious nearby.

Movement flickers inside the house, and then the door swings open.

Truly beams when she sees me, and pulls me in for a hug. "Loveday," she says over my shoulder. "What a surprise."

"Hi. I hope this is okay."

We break apart. "Of course. Any time."

She closes the door behind us, locking it in place. Turning to me, she pushes some of her shoulder-length, golden blond hair behind her ear. "Come on in." She leads me through to her kitchen, a white, marble affair with brass accents and a large bouquet of flowers bursting out of a bright green vase in the middle of the island workspace.

I slide onto one of the bar stools, folding my hands on the counter.

"Can I get you anything? I just made some blueberry scones."

My eyes light up. "I used to love those!"

"It's providential," Truly says, lifting a large, gleaming gold tin and setting it in front of me. "Help yourself. I'll get us something to drink." She pours two tall glasses of ice-cold milk and slips onto the stool beside mine.

I open the tin and the warm smell of sugary baked goods lifts toward my nose. I let out a groan. "I don't know what you're going to eat, but every single one of these scones is mine."

Truly's laugh tinkles. Her bright blue eyes find mine. "What brings you for a visit? I'm guessing it's not a physics question."

I smile, munching on my scone. After swallowing my bite, I speak. "You've known my dad forever, right?"

Her cheeks turn a rosy pink. "I met him the day before I started teaching you and Antonia. Um, I mean Clarity. He came to size me up, and see who the CIA had hired to teach his kids." She takes a bite of her scone, chewing thoughtfully.

"And you knew he was a spy."

She laughs again, covering her mouth with a slender hand. "I didn't know for sure. The lady who hired me didn't say anything like that. She simply said that some of the CIA's employees would prefer a more private education for their children. They paid me a pittance, but it was my first teaching job, and I loved it."

"But my dad, what was he like?"

Truly's warm eyes meet mine. "He was quiet, serious, and totally at a loss as to what to do with the two five-year-old rascals he was raising." She reaches out and puts a gentle hand on my arm. "He loved you two more than anything. He still does." Her smile softens and her gaze goes hazy. Snapping out of it, she takes a quick sip of her milk.

It occurs to me that she sounds more sentimental than just a family teacher, but I'd have known if she and my dad had been more than teacher and parent, right? Pushing that surprising thought away, I speak. "Did it bother you that you knew so little about the parents of your students?"

She shakes her head, her blond hair shining. "No. I understood the reason behind their secrecy, and I had a job to do. I was too busy having a blast with you kids to worry about that."

I bite my lip. "But, how did you trust them? The adults?"

Truly looks at me as if she knows there's more behind my question than I'm saying, like there's someone behind my question, but I don't volunteer the information. My eyes sink toward my lap.

Truly tilts her head, thinking about this. "Hmm... We all have instincts, right? And sometimes they tell us that something is off with a person. I think it's wise to pay attention to those feelings. But sometimes instincts tell you a person is good and trustworthy. I listen to those feelings too, until someone proves otherwise. People will show you who they are by their actions, and when they do, you can believe them."

"So basically, you're saying you went with your gut."

She nods. "I guess I am." Her gray-blue eyes find mine, and a smile flits over her features. "Is there someone your gut is telling you is untrustworthy?"

I frown, wringing my hands in my lap. "My gut says he's trustworthy, that he could be… But I found out he was keeping something big from me, and I hate that."

The corners of Truly's mouth pull down. "Was it something bad?"

I give a slight shake of my head. "Not bad, really, just surprising."

"And you got mad about it."

My eyes widen at her succinct estimation of me.

Seeing my expression, Truly puts an arm around me. "You were always one of my most inquisitive students. You wanted to know everything. You never liked being kept in the dark."

Her smile returns. "And from the looks of it, that hasn't changed."

"It's just, I thought we were getting close, but then I found out this thing… and I don't know if I can get past it," I finish, exhaling.

She pats my shoulder before lowering her arm. "You're a smart, strong, insightful girl. If you want to get to know this person better, and forgive him for not telling you this thing, whatever it is, you'll be able to do it. I have faith in you."

My entire body warms at this. It's been a long time since I've had a heart to heart with Truly, and it's surprising how nice it feels. "Thank you."

Truly gives my shoulder a squeeze before withdrawing her hand. "Why don't you have another scone?"

I grin, reaching into the tin and taking another pastry. "Don't mind if I do."

My resolve to be angry at Starling forever starts to melt as I nibble my scone. From what I've seen so far, Starling is the epitome of honest. Truly is right; if Starling didn't want me to know he was Charles Darnay's son, he must have had a good reason.

Chapter 17

The tile floor of the bathroom is slick as I step out of the shower and wrap a towel around myself. The fan whirrs in its spot on the ceiling, working to lower the humidity in the room. I swing the metal stall door open and cross to the mirror, swiping at the steam that's covering the glass. It's no use. Beads of condensation slip down the mirror, making it impossible to see my reflection.

I brush my teeth as I wait, watching the mirror as it clears. That's when I see it.

A loud screech rends my lips, tearing through the quiet evening in the Tower.

My hair is bright green.

The lights in the control room are dim as I rush inside, eyes swiveling in search of a boy with a death wish. The great screen at the front of the room is dark. Haru, alone, is there, hunched over her laptop.

I clear my throat to announce my presence.

"Loveday!" Haru beams from her seat, where a blueprint glows on her laptop screen. "Guess what I just found?" She pushes off from the desk, spinning her chair to face me. At the sight of my hair, her eyes go wide. "Lotus?" she asks.

"He's a dead man."

"It looks… nice," she stammers.

"Sure. You were saying?"

"Guess what I found?" Her voice is more timid now, as if her surprise isn't as important now that I've got green hair, but I don't let it faze me.

"The blueprints for CIA headquarters?"

She winks at me. "Bingo."

I rub my hands together. "Excellent. We'll take a look at it later, all right?"

Haru's head bobs in vigorous agreement. There's a fuschia-colored, faux fur scrunchie wrapped around her ponytail. "That's fine with me. I need to go on an errand, anyway." She hops out of her seat, scoops her laptop into her arms, and skips from the room.

Music from the *Pirates of the Caribbean* soundtrack swells through the door to Royal's office, making me smile. He must be in a good mood. Perfect. Squaring my shoulders, I wait until the crescendo coming from inside quiets, and then I rap on the wooden surface with sharp knuckles.

"Come in," he says in an easy voice.

The volume of the music lowers to a hush.

"It's me," I say as I push the door open and step inside. With one hand, I close it behind me without a sound.

Royal's eyebrows rise at the sight of my grinchy green hair. "Don't you think this prank war with Lotus is getting out of hand?" He can't hide the amusement in his voice or the twinkle in his eyes.

"I'm only getting started."

As if on cue, the security system starts blaring the synthesized pop song. *"Spin me on the dance floor, spin me again…"*

I glance down at my watch. "Huh."

"What is it now?" Royal asks, a resigned look on his face.

"Haru just left the Tower. I'm not sure why the system is playing the song now."

He leans forward, interlacing his fingers over the surface of his airplane wing desk. "I thought I told you to fix it."

My brows furrow. "I did. I had her go into the system and reset it, so it should beep like normal when someone comes or goes." Reaching up, I run a hand through my hair, pushing it off my forehead.

"Clearly, it didn't work," my dad says with a sigh.

"I'll try it again." I sink down into the chair opposite his desk and fix my gaze on him.

"Is there something you want to talk to me about?"

I purse my lips, not sure how to continue. He knows about my intention to visit Aunt Megan while she's in custody, but I'm still not sure how he'll receive it. He wasn't a fan of the idea, to put it mildly.

Biting my lip, I push ahead. "I went to see Aunt Megan, in Baltimore."

He doesn't blink as he looks at me.

"It wasn't what I expected. Prison is… cold. And really intense."

A slight nod.

"Look, she said something that threw me. I don't know if you knew, and you're keeping it from me, or if…" A tinge of frustration rises in me. If he's keeping more secrets from me, I don't know what I'll do. But it won't be pretty. "But then Truly said to give you the benefit of the doubt, so that's what I'm trying to do."

My knees bounce in my chair.

"Truly? What did she… Never mind. What do you want to ask me?"

"My aunt Megan said my maternal grandparents are still alive. Did you know?"

But his shocked expression makes it obvious that he didn't know. He's astonished, just like I was. "Haven't you ever looked in on them?" I ask. "Even via satellite?"

He runs a hand over his jaw, shaking his head. "After your mom died…" Royal's voice cracks. He inhales through his nose and tries again. "After she died, I saw them at the funeral. They were furious. They blamed me, and I couldn't justify myself to them. We didn't speak after that day. Time passed, and I found it was easier not to think about them. It never occurred to me that after sixteen years they were still alive."

I sag in my chair. He's telling the truth. "They never asked about me?"

A muscle in Royal's jaw ticks. "They sent you birthday cards for a couple of years. I gave them to you, but you were so little, you probably don't remember. After the first three or four years, the cards stopped coming, and I assumed—"

"You assumed they were dead."

The sad look in his eyes confirms this.

I stand, running both hands through my hair. "What do I do now? Should I go see them? Do you think they'd want to see me?"

Royal gives me a piercing look with his ocean blue eyes. "You can't go see them."

The words settle in the air between us.

I swallow. "Because of my job."

"It's one of the main reasons I didn't try to repair my relationship with them after your mother passed. I didn't want to endanger them."

My heart skips a beat. "You think I've made enemies who will come looking for a way to hurt me?"

"With Beppe Arnoni behind bars, and many of his men dead, I'd guess you're safe for now, but if you continue in this line of work, making enemies is not unlikely."

"But Aunt Megan wasn't a spy, and she's the only one who's ever come after you." A note of pleading threads its way into my voice.

He leans back in his chair, appraising me. "That isn't true."

I open my mouth to question him, but he holds up a hand.

"I've shielded you from it," he continues, "but why do you think I moved us down here into an impregnable concrete fortress?"

I freeze at this. "You were hiding from someone?"

Royal shakes his head. "Not any one person, but after you girls started working in the field, I knew it was a matter of time before someone who was angry with me would try to get to me through you. It just took a few more years than I expected." He gives a half-hearted laugh at this.

I sink into my chair, my stomach clenched in disappointment. "Okay, I won't go see them."

"I know it's hard," my dad says, "but it's for the best."

He may be right, but that doesn't prevent it from feeling like another in a long line of losses.

Chapter 18

Clarity's makeup is strewn all over the floor when I get back to our room. She's peering into the mirror, holding an eyeliner pencil in her hand.

"Whatcha doing?" I ask, leaning against the doorframe.

She leans closer to the mirror, eyeing the lines of her face. "Trying to decide the best way to make myself into a mermaid."

I snort. "Practicing again?"

"Of course." She swivels to look at me with a grin on her face and her eyes lit. "Can I do you?"

I lean away from her, hesitating. "Actually, I was hoping you'd come help me with something."

Her eyebrow arches. "Like what?"

One corner of my mouth lifts. I put a hand into the pocket of my trench coat and pull out a roll of cling wrap. "Payback."

She smiles. "For your hair? Which we need to fix, by the way."

I nod.

"Let's go."

Forty minutes later we're stretched out on the floor of the den playing a card game. Several empty rolls of cling wrap sit discarded in the dumpster behind the hotel.

Lotus and Julep stroll out of the dormitory, dropping their intertwined fingers before they think I catch a glimpse of them. They're both clad head to toe in black leather and heavy denim. It appears a motorcycle ride is on the agenda.

Perfect.

I feign ignorance, looking up to meet their eyes.

Beside me, Clarity's mouth curves in a pleasant, and not at all mischievous, smile.

"What's up?" I ask, my eyes floating down to the cards in my hand. I bite my lip, pretending to be deep in the process of deciding which one to play.

Lotus scratches his neck. "You guys hungry? Julep and I are thinking about going out for some Italian food or something."

I put a card on the stack, and then hold the rest against my chest. "Your turn," I tell my sister.

She nods, her own eyes hopping between the couple standing over us and the cards cradled in her fingers.

I glance between Lotus and Julep's legs and catch a glimpse of Starling striding toward us. He opens his mouth to speak, but Clarity gives him a warning look.

Starling's lips come together in confusion.

I meet my sister's eyes, and she shakes her head. She slaps her card down on the pile. "Uno!"

"No way!" I protest. "Hey, you hungry? Want to take a break?"

She shakes her head. "When I'm winning? Not on your life."

Turning to Lotus and Julep, I say, "No, thanks, we're good. You guys feel free to go out, though."

"We'll find something here," Clarity puts in.

Starling skirts around the couple and plops down beside us. "Yes, we'll find something here." He glances at me, a question in his eyes.

I wink at him.

His eyebrows rise, but then his face relaxes into a smile. He knows something is up.

"Alrighty then," Lotus says. He takes his helmet and a spare off the hooks by the door. Handing one to Julep, he gestures for her to go ahead of him down the service tunnel to the parking garage.

In a minute, they're gone and the heavy concrete door has slid closed behind them.

"Okay," Starling asks. "What's going on?"

I grin. "Wait a second. You'll see." My cards hang forgotten in my hand as I listen.

The security system ramps up, projecting that insipid song into the Ivory Tower.

I groan, pushing to stand up.

Clarity puts a hand on my leg. "Wait for it."

Lotus storms into the Tower, a look of disbelief on his face. "You saran wrapped my motorcycle? Do you know how long it'll take to get that off?"

Clarity and I dissolve into laughter.

"Gotcha."

Lotus's head bobs "Oh. Okay. The green hair wasn't enough, huh? Okay." He rubs his hands together, and then points at me. "I'ma fix my bike, and then I'm coming for you."

"Sure," I retort. "Hit me with your best shot."

"Wait," Starling puts in, a hand on my shoulder. "You did what to his bike?"

"I helped," Clarity adds.

"Come and see," Lotus says. "It's an act of war."

We all trot along the service tunnel and emerge into the covered parking garage.

Julep waves at us from where she's standing in the corner under the glow of a harsh orange light, a hand over her mouth to smother her laughter.

Next to her stands Lotus's parked motorcycle.

And it's covered from stem to stern in cling wrap.

Nobody's riding that sucker anywhere tonight.

"Why don't y'all come with us to dinner?" Julep asks as she walks toward us, her black booties slapping the pavement.

I glance at Lotus, who plasters on a fake smile. "Sure, come with us."

Julep nudges him with her elbow, and he meets her eyes. They have an unspoken conversation, and then she turns to face the three of us. "We're going for Italian. Sound good?"

Clarity stretches her arms wide, groaning softly. "That does sound nice. I'm in."

I roll my shoulders. "I could use the walk. We're walking, right?"

"Give me a minute," Starling says, jogging back into the Tower. In a minute, he returns with Haru, who's pulling her hoodie on over her head. "We're going out? That sounds great!"

Lotus shakes his head at my cheshire cat grin. "You're smiling now," he says. "Just wait." He throws an arm around Julep's shoulders, and the two of them lead the way out of the parking garage toward the road.

Bold move.

On the street, it's peak traffic time. Cars trundle past us on the road, pressing the cars ahead of them to move just a little faster. As if any of them could influence the slow speed of the evening traffic.

Lotus and Julep set the pace, leading our pack up the block toward downtown.

Clarity and Haru skip after them, gleeful at being outside in the fresh air.

I follow, enjoying the free movement of my limbs in the cool evening.

Starling brings up the rear, the sounds of his footfalls on the pavement right behind mine.

Beside us, a car blasts its horn.

I spin toward it, my guard up, but the driver isn't looking at my team. He's making angry faces at the car ahead of him, gesticulating with his hands.

"Someone's out of sorts this evening," Starling whispers, sliding into step with me.

"No kidding."

He walks shoulder to shoulder with me, keeping his hand at his side.

My skin warms at his nearness, but I resist the urge to take his hand. After all, I was the one who blurted, truthfully, that I barely know him. I've enjoyed getting to know him over the past couple weeks, but there's still so much more to learn before I'm ready to jump into a relationship, or whatever it was we were involved in.

I look up at him, at his sharp cheekbones and dark eyes.

"You're staring," he says, turning his gaze toward me.

"Just looking."

His mouth twists into a half smile.

"Got me all figured out yet?"

"Not even close."

He chuckles. He returns his focus to the sidewalk ahead of us, his countenance thoughtful. "Italian food always reminds me of my aunt."

Eager to listen, I incline my head toward him. "Yeah? How come?"

"Well, you know she raised me while my dad was away building his hotel empire."

"Right."

"As a kid, I was desperate to spend some real time with my dad, so one year when he asked me what I wanted for my birthday, I told him I wanted to take a trip. He asked me where, and Italy was the first country that came to mind." He laughs softly.

"What did he say?"

"He was surprised, but he agreed to take me. He said he just had to take a quick business trip first." He stops, his expression darkening.

"He didn't make it back, did he?"

Starling looks at me again. "No." His mouth puckers around the word, as if its utterance is accompanied by the bitter taste of disappointment.

"So what happened?"

"My aunt took one look at me and got on the phone. You should have heard her. She yelled at my dad something fierce, and then she took me to Italy herself. We saw everything—the Coliseum, the Vatican, Pompeii—and I ate so much pizza and pasta I thought I'd explode. It was brilliant." He's smiling now.

"That sounds amazing," I say, my heart warming at his smile.

He fixes his dark eyes on me. "What about you? Did you take any memorable trips as a kid?"

"One summer, the three of us did a road trip across the U.S., visiting national parks. We started in Acadia and ended up at the Redwood National Park in California. We slept in a tiny, two-person tent. It was crammed, but Clarity and I loved it, especially all the spaghetti o's we ate." I laugh at the memory. "I haven't had those in years."

"Maybe they'll have some at the restaurant." He gestures ahead of us, where Lotus, Julep, Clarity, and Haru are standing on the sidewalk outside the Italian place. "And here we are."

Inside, the restaurant is lit with large, wrought iron chandeliers. Arches span the ceiling, separating different eating areas to make them feel smaller and cozier.

Lotus steps up to the counter. Scratching at his neck, he speaks to the waiting hostess. "Um, I have a reservation, but there are six of us now instead of two." He leans closer to her and whispers something I can't make out.

The hostess's smile doesn't waver. "No problem."

We're led to a private booth to one side of the dining area.

There's a waiter clearing a bouquet of red roses off the table as we approach.

Julep looks at Lotus and back at the waiter. "Were those for me?"

Lotus blushes. "Yeah."

Haru lets out a high-pitched, "Aww."

Julep snaps them out of the waiter's hands, lifting them to her nose and inhaling their scent. "They smell heavenly." She beams at Lotus, who shifts on his feet.

"The florist said they smell the best," he says with a bashful smile. His eyes cut toward me.

"Chill, man. I already knew you two were a thing."

Lotus's body sags in relief. "Thank goodness. I'm so tired of faking." He slides into the burgundy leather booth beside Julep and puts an arm across the back of the seat behind her.

Clarity slides into the middle beside Julep, followed by Haru, me, and then Starling.

"I hear the veal here is delicious," Julep says, poring over

115

her menu.

But we don't get the chance to taste it.

Literally, the minute our food arrives, artfully displayed on gleaming white plates, all of our watches buzz.

Royal
Where are you?
Get back to the Tower.
STAT

We meet each other's gazes across the table.

"That can't be good," Julep says, shaking her head.

"STAT messages are never good," Lotus adds, flagging down the waiter and asking for to-go boxes.

With brown takeout bags in hand, we're out the door, our feet slamming over the pavement as we sprint back to the hotel.

My stomach is in a knot as dread overtakes me. What could prompt such an urgent message from Royal, who's normally so calm and collected? Whatever it is, it can't be good.

Chapter 19

The electronic bump of that grating pop song is already thumping when we step into the Tower.

I glance at Haru, who blanches. "I'm sorry! I've tried resetting the system twice already I don't know what the problem is."

My lips purse. "We'll have to try again. We're already strung tight as it is."

She nods. "Okay."

We shrug off our coats and hang them on the hooks lining the door to the den.

Lotus and Julep add their motorcycle helmets to the rack, and we all shuffle toward the control room, the tantalizing scent of hot Italian food lingering around us.

Royal is standing in the dimly lit room, rubbing at his eyes with one hand. "Can someone shut off this wretched music?" he growls.

Haru squeaks and scrambles into her desk chair. "I'll try." Whipping her laptop out of her crossbody bag, she flips it open and starts typing. In the corner of her screen, a small window shows a view into her parents' living room. She's been checking on them more often lately.

My lips tighten as I take a seat. I've been thinking about asking Royal to send her home for a few days, after our op at CIA headquarters.

The rest of my teammates take seats around the table, opening our biodegradable food containers and eating our food in silence. The smells of melted cheese and creamy sauces make my mouth water.

The pounding of the baseline in the music seems to grow louder, until there's a headache threatening behind my eyes.

"Some prank this turned into," Lotus says, shooting an admonishing look my way.

"Never again."

"Just for tonight, baby, baby, one more dance. Take me to the dance floor, spin—"

It cuts off abruptly, the sound dying as the speakers go silent.

Haru sags in her chair and spins to face us, relief spreading over her face.

"Finally," Royal says, voice gruff. Pulling out the nearest chair, he takes it and scoots in, folding his arms on the tabletop. "We've got a problem."

The words cut through the air, cranking up the tension in the room.

My shoulders draw together, and I set down my fork. "What kind of problem?"

Royal shifts his gaze toward me, his cool blue eyes heavy. "There's been an incident at CIA headquarters. An employee tried to get into the server room without clearance, by attempting to hack into the facial recognition software."

My eyebrows rise. "After their cyber security guy was found dead? That's probably not a coincidence."

Royal shakes his head, face grim.

I wipe my mouth on my napkin. "How did he get access?"

"It looks like Ray Parks tried to create a backdoor in the system, before he passed. The employee they caught today was attempting to use the facial scanner to unlock the server room under another employee's name. It appears that Ray Parks uploaded this man's photo to another person's profile in order to trick the scanner."

"Did it work?"

"No, but it might have if he hadn't been interrupted."

I take a bite of my ravioli, considering this.

Royal continues. "The CIA believes Nexus is behind the attack today, and they're suspicious he also has something to do with the death of Ray Parks."

"Of course he did," Starling says. "Think about it. If Nexus wasn't involved, we're saying that Ray Parks created a way to work around the security it was his job to shore up, and then he killed himself."

"Yeah, being put in jail for treason would be rough, but at least you'd still be alive," Lotus mumbles around a bite of pasta.

Julep takes a big bite, and her eyes widen. "Hot, hot," she mutters, fanning herself with her hand. She jumps out of her chair and bolts out of the room.

The gurgle of water running through the pipes draws my eyes upward to the concrete ceiling, where the industrial lights hang over the table.

We remain silent. We'll continue the discussion once she returns.

I focus on eating my lobster ravioli, one small bite at a time. They didn't give me as much food as I would have liked, so I'm trying to savor it. As I chew, I mull over the events over the past few days. First Ray Parks, and now some other guy?

Julep strides into the room with an arm full of water

119

bottles. She hands them out before resuming her seat.

"Thank you," Lotus says, grinning at her. "Eat slower, will you?"

She smiles sheepishly, smoothing her skirt with her hands.

"So let me get this straight," Lotus says. "First, Ray Parks creates a way to get into the CIA's system without having the required clearance codes, and then he dies."

"And then, someone else uses that same hack to try to get into the room where he'd have access to all of the CIA's top secret files," Clarity says, balancing her bottle cap on the tip of her finger.

"Obviously, the facial recognition software is not bulletproof. And Nexus knows it. The question is, what does he want with those files? And why not pay Ray Parks to steal them?"

All eyes are on me now.

"Both good questions," Royal says, gaze leveled at me. "In the meantime, the CIA is already combing through their facial recognition software, making sure all of their employee's accounts match their photos."

I swivel to face Haru. "We need to confirm that someone paid Ray Parks to create the back door. With all that gambling debt, he might be persuaded. We need to look into his emails, text messages, recent call log. Maybe there's something we missed."

"Were there any large deposits on his bank statements?" Starling asks. "It might be worth revisiting those."

Royal glances at Haru.

"On it," she says, concentrating on her laptop screen.

"I don't remember seeing any transactions that sent up a red flag," Julep says, "but then again, we weren't looking at his deposits last time."

"Maybe he grew a conscience and refused to go through with it," Lotus says. "It could happen."

I nod slowly. "Maybe." Turning to Royal, I lean forward. "What about the guy they caught today. Have they questioned him yet?"

"Aha!" Haru exclaims. "About six weeks ago, Ray Parks received a money transfer of $100,000. He moved most of it to an investment account."

"Can you trace the transfer back to the sender?"

Haru bites her lip in concentration. "I can try."

Royal's mouth sets in a grim line. "The man they took into custody today is refusing to cooperate."

"Shocker. I wouldn't talk either if I had someone like Nexus pulling my strings."

"I spoke to Gillian Harris a few minutes ago," Royal continues.

An eager thrill runs through me.

"I take it Ms. Harris agreed to give the team another chance at their system?" Julep asks.

Royal's grim expression doesn't change. "She did."

I pump my fist, and Lotus lets out a whoop.

"Looks like it's a good thing the CIA agreed to a second try," Julep continues. "And none too soon."

"Indeed," Starling adds.

"I finally found those blueprints, this afternoon," Haru puts in. With a flick of her wrist on her touchscreen, the plans fill the giant screen at the front of the room. "I've put a yellow dot on the server room, where we need to get to. It's in the basement, of course. And I've put red dots on all of the exterior doors and windows."

"Gimme those," I say, holding out my greedy hands for her tablet.

Haru complies, passing the device over to me.

In the next chair, Lotus peers at the screen over my shoulder. "Looks like there are lots of ways in." He runs fidgety fingers over his afro.

"I have a feeling getting inside will be the easy part," Clarity says. "Just like last time. It'll be getting out that's the problem."

Starling's eyes slide toward mine, still smiling. "Do you think you can handle this?" he asks. "I'm happy to trade places."

I give a slow head shake. "This op is mine." My eyes skim over the blueprints, looking for the best points of ingress and egress. Then I see it: the spot where their security will likely be weakest. I'm confident when I say, "There's a hole in their security, and I'm going to use it."

I could definitely fall asleep like this. I'm stretched out on the cool countertop with a towel rolled under my neck, and my head hanging backward into the kitchen sink. Clarity stands over me, massaging shampoo into my hair, which is still an unflattering verdigris hue. Her graceful fingers roll over my scalp, lulling me into a fully relaxed state.

Clarity says something, but I don't catch it.

"What?"

She laughs. "Enjoying this, are you? I was just saying that, if you want, we could dye your hair a different color for a change."

I respond without opening my eyes. "No, I'll stick with the blond. Thanks, though."

"My pleasure." She goes on rubbing small circles through my hair with her fingers, and I slip toward sleep.

A poke to the center of my stomach sets my instincts humming, and I spring upward into a squat on the countertop, ready to spring at my attacker. My water-saturated hair feels slimy on my neck as the conditioner runs down the strands and soaks the top of my black tank top.

Lotus busts up laughing, one hand over his mouth. "You should see your face right now," he cackles. "You look so scared." He mimics my fearful expression, the glee of his successful sneak attack making him bounce on the balls of his feet. "You weren't expecting that, were you?"

At my back, Clarity hums in agreement.

My eyes narrow at him as my mouth quirks up. "If I weren't already killing you in a prank war, I'd—"

"Excuse me? Who is killing who here?" One hand rises to his muscled chest in effrontery. "I think it's me who's doing the killing."

"Tell yourself that if it helps you sleep at night."

Clarity huffs, wrapping her fingers around my wrist and giving a gentle tug. "Get down here. You're dripping conditioner all over the place."

"Fine, but warn me next time, will you?" I glance up at her as I lay down on the counter with only my feet hanging off the edge.

Lotus swings the fridge open and rests one hand on the top of its door so he can lean into the cool interior. "What have we got in here that's good?" After some rummaging, he emerges with a soda. "Catch you two later." The drink fizzes once he pops the top open, the sound lingering even after Lotus jogs up the stairs.

Turning the faucet to warm water, Clarity begins rinsing out my hair, alternating running her fingers through it and squeezing it to remove excess water.

"I should have you wash my hair every time," I mumble, my eyes lifting to catch hers.

She smiles. "You couldn't afford me."

"Is that so? How about you do it as my birthday present."

My sister titters. "I already have your present, but someone else was asking me for ideas." Her smile is coy.

"Starling."

"Mmhm."

I let my gaze rise to the ceiling, thinking it over. "I guess I could use a gift certificate to the movies. I haven't been to the theater in ages. And maybe some candy to go with it?"

Clarity nukes a hand towel in the microwave just long enough to make it toasty warm, and then she rings out my hair and wraps the warm terry cloth around it. The heat from the towel seeps into my neck, making me even more sleepy than the scalp massage. "I'll tell him."

I pull up to a seated position on the counter, my legs dangling off the edge. The warmth from the towel fades as I rub my hair.

"Can you believe you're turning eighteen in thirty-six hours? How does it feel to be almost an adult?"

"Honestly? I've felt like an adult since I was twelve and we did our first bump and grab."

Clarity's eyes fall, her smile not reaching her eyes. "Me too."

I shift from my back to my side, running my fingers through my still-damp hair, but my mind won't shut up. There's still something bothering me about today's attempted breach at the CIA. If Nexus was behind it, can we really assume he wants the NOC list? And what will he do if he gets his hands on it?

Royal said he was responsible for several agent deaths almost twenty years ago, but what would make him surface again now? Something must have kept him from coming out of hiding for the past decade and a half.

A frustrated sigh escapes me, and I flop onto my back.

Sheets rustle down below.

"Loveday?" Clarity whispers into the dark. "Are you awake?"

"Yeah. What's up?" I reach up to fluff my pillow, and then squish my head into the down.

"I talked to my uncle today." Her words are slow, hesitant.

My chest tightens. "Yeah? Good."

"He said he told his wife and daughter about me… They want to meet me. He said they're pretty excited." Her words are slow, hesitant, as if she's not sure how I'm going to react.

I gulp down the jealousy that rises into my throat. I'm used to being Clarity's number one, but lately I've felt supplanted by her Uncle Nestore. Even though I know he wasn't responsible for her kidnapping, I can't help the suspicion that creeps in whenever my sister mentions him.

"Loveday?"

I realize I've been silent for too long. "Sorry. Just thinking."

This time, Clarity is quiet, waiting for me to continue.

I open my mouth to speak, but clamp it shut again. There are so many things I could say, should say, but my words lay thick in my throat.

Finally, I push my quilt off and sit up so I can peer down at my sister, even though I can't see her below me in our dark room. "I'm not sure Roy—Dad will go for it. He may say you'd be putting them at risk, and yourself."

Clarity huffs. "Don't you think they're used to risk, since

their patriarch was a *mob boss*?"

"Maybe, but still…"

"Can't you talk to him, convince him?"

Again I fall silent, my thoughts wandering to my mom's parents, grandparents I've never met, never seen in photos. I don't even know their names. "My grandparents are still alive," I breathe.

"What?!" Clarity shrieks, and then continues quieter. "Are you going to visit them?"

I shake my head, sinking onto my pillow. "Royal forbade it. He said it would put them in danger, and compromise me, too."

"Oh." The realization in my sister's voice cuts me to the quick, making my heart sting.

"I'm sorry." The words are little more than a whisper.

She doesn't respond, but I think I hear a sniffle from below.

My eyes start to prick, but I bite my tongue to force quit.

It doesn't happen often, but this is one of those times I almost wish we were a typical civilian family, instead of what we are.

Chapter 20

Under my pillow, a Radish Head song starts playing from the tiny speaker on my watch. The down feathers muffle the music, but it's still enough to wake me up. I drag my hand out from under the pillowcase and look at the time.

My stomach drops.

I'm supposed to be in the control center by 7:25, and it's already 07:15. I must've hit the snooze button a few times.

Scrambling to unwind my body from my twisted sheets, I kick them off and jump down from my bed, landing on the floor with a thump that wakes Clarity.

She sits up and pushes her sleeping mask up her forehead. "What time is it?" she moans, smacking her dry lips.

"Go back to sleep," I whisper. "You don't have to report this morning, remember?"

With a relieved "Mmm," she snuggles down in her blankets, snapping her lavender scented mask into place.

I tiptoe around the room, dressing as quickly as I can in the dark, with only the tiny beam of light from my watch to guide me. I pull on a pair of black leggings, a charcoal gray tunic shirt, and an oversized, navy pullover sweater. My usual black tennis shoes envelop my feet. I shine the minute beam over Clarity's wigs, weighing my options. Finally, I select a wig of curly black hair that will billow around my shoulders and make my green eyes pop.

My watch vibrates.

Starling
Where are you?

I've got five minutes to be in the control room.

Me
One minute.

Starling
!

I pull a wig cap out of one of the drawers in Clarity's vanity, pulling it expertly onto my head. I'll put the wig on in the bathroom, where I can see what I'm doing.

I creep across the room and run my hands along the flat door panel, fumbling for the knob. My fingers slap the cool metal. With a twist, I pull open the door.

The stench of bleach assaults my nostrils, making me recoil into my room.

Behind me, Clarity gags as the malodorous air coats our bedroom. "What IS that?"

My eyes fall to the floor in shock and awe.

There must be a hundred red plastic cups spread strategically across the floor, only two inches apart. And each one is filled almost to the brim with the clear, stinking liquid.

Across the hall, there's a narrow strip of floor that's devoid of the bleach-filled cups. It's a walking path that allows everyone but me to exit the dormitory.

Lotus is leaning against Haru's door, arms crossed, a self-satisfied smile on his face. "Good morning," he says. "It's about time you showed your face. Like my handiwork?" he sweeps one hand over the expanse of the hallway.

"How am I supposed to get out of here? I have to be in the control room in—" I look down at my watch. "Two minutes."

Lotus's grin widens. "Very carefully." Then he saunters down the hallway, giving a loud hoot of pleasure before he disappears into the den.

Clarity leans over my shoulder, peering down at the floor. "Bleach cups, huh?"

"Mmhm."

She tilts her head to look at me. "Want me to throw you across?"

"I'm not a frisbee."

She shrugs before flipping the light switch to illuminate our room. "Then I suggest you find another way out, quick."

At my wrist, my watch vibrates.

Starling
You coming?

Me
I'm trapped behind a barricade of bleach cups.

Starling
I was wondering what those were for.

Me
And you didn't think to clear them away from my door?

Starling
It's a prank war.

129

I am not getting involved.

I don't bother to respond. "Wish me luck."

"Good luck," my sister chirps as she takes the wig out of my hand. "I'll hand it to you once you're across."

I take a few steps back to give myself space, and take a running leap toward Haru's bedroom door. My body slams into it, causing my brain to rattle in my skull.

Inside, Haru lets loose a blood-curdling scream.

I fall back, managing to catch myself on my hands. Clear, cold liquid runs over my fingers, and I twist around to survey the damage. I've knocked over seven cups of bleach, and the carpet is already starting to discolor.

Haru opens her door a crack. "What's going on? Are we under attack?"

I glare up at her. "Does it look like it?"

She scans the hallway before settling her eyes on me. "What are you doing?"

"What does it look like?" I snap, regretting my tone the instant the words hit our ears.

Haru frowns and starts to duck into her room.

"Wait! I'm sorry. This isn't your fault."

She reappears between her door and its frame. "Did Lotus do this?" she asks, sniffing at the foul odor.

"Yep."

Haru reaches down to help me up, but one word makes us freeze.

"Loveday."

My blood chills. I already know what I'll see, but I look anyway.

Royal is standing in the entrance to the dormitory with his arms crossed firmly over his chest, and the look he's giving me would make anybody with an iota of self-preservation instinct run in the other direction.

Unluckily for me, my retreat is blocked by an army of bleach cups.

And stained carpet.

Yay.

The parking lot in front of CIA headquarters is bustling with people as they arrive for the start of their workday. In mere minutes, the lot goes from basically empty to teaming with cars. Doors open and slam shut. Shoes slap or clack against the pavement as men and women of all shapes and sizes make their way into the buildings, carrying suitcases, purses, lunch boxes, and umbrellas.

The pavement is soggy from the torrent of rain that soaked the grounds during the night, and gray clouds rumble overhead, threatening to unleash further waterworks.

From our vantage point inside Royal's Civic, Starling and I sit relaxed in our seats, appearing as if we belong in this parking lot as much as any other person who's here.

Never mind that we've been here for two hours, as indicated by the fast food wrappers that are crinkled up and bunched in a mound on the center console.

Starling takes a deep breath. "What's our next move?"

I crane my neck, watching the stragglers hustle into the buildings, the glass doors swinging closed behind them. "Once everyone is inside, we'll take a walk around the grounds. If anyone stops us, we'll say we're here to see the museum and memorial garden. In my experience, adults love teenagers who are interested in art and history."

Over the comms, Royal grunts.

"It's true, isn't it?"

He mumbles something I can't make out.

"And are you?" Starling asks, his brown eyes sliding to mine. "Interested in those things?"

My lips bunch to one side. "I don't have a lot of experience with art, but I do enjoy reading about history. The machinations of the different country's leaders and governments are intriguing."

He bobs his head. "I wouldn't have guessed you were a history buff."

I rest my head against the headrest, not taking my eyes off his. "Did I say anything about being a buff? No, I did not. I simply said that political intrigue interests me. That's not the same thing."

His lips curl into a placating smile. "Next time I'm stumped by a history question on a crossword puzzle, I'll know who to ask."

"By all means." I take a sip of my formerly steaming hot cocoa, which is now lukewarm, but still creamy and sweet. "Mmm, this was a good call."

Starling's smile widens. "I'm glad you like it."

Using a napkin, I swipe at my lips to make sure I don't have a brown cocoa mustache. "So why do you do crosswords, anyway?"

My companion's fingers fidget with the seam of his styrofoam cup, and he gazes out across the parking lot. "My mom did them. She saved every single crossword from the newspaper, and worked on them in the evenings. At least, that's what my dad told me when I was little. I found a stack of unfinished ones in his dresser once, but the next time I looked, they were gone."

"You do them for her."

Starling's eyes find mine again, his voice low. "Is that silly?"

"Not at all." I swallow, licking my lips. My words are hesitant when I speak. "How did she die?"

Starling's expression clouds over, and he waits so long to speak that I'm not sure he's going to answer. His lips part, and the words squeeze out. His breathing is shallow, as if every breath brings pain. "We were in the park. I was two, and she was watching me go down the slide. Apparently, I liked to do it over and over again, and each time I'd reach the top of the stairs, I'd yell, "Watch me, Mum!" At least, that's what my aunt told me. We were there one day, me on the slide and my mum sitting on one of the benches facing the playground, and someone shot her." His voice cracks. "I don't remember it, but my aunt told me that the police found me clinging to the railing at the top of the play equipment, crying and screaming for my mum to "Watch me!" Only, she couldn't. She was dead. She bled out on that park bench." He falls silent, and my heart wrenches in my chest.

There's a quiet gasp over the comms. Royal again.

I don't know what to say. "I'm so sorry." It's not enough.

Starling's mouth tightens into a thin line, and he blinks a few times.

My stomach is churning in my belly. I don't know if it'll help at all, but fair is fair. "My mom died in a car crash, and I was in the back seat. My parents got into a fight, about Clarity, actually, and my mom packed a bag. She was going to take me to stay with my aunt for a few days—yes, the one you met in St. Petersburg—but it had been raining and the roads were a mess. She lost control and rammed straight into a broken guardrail." I cringe at the words, images of a crumpled car with a shattered windshield flashing through my mind's eye. The blood on the glass. The gurney carrying a body covered in a white sheet. The empty infant car seat, untouched by the horror taking place in the driver's seat.

Starling's eyes are wide and full of sympathy. "You were in the car?"

"I was mere feet away, and I didn't have a scratch on me. But she… she died on impact."

In a slow, tentative movement, Starling reaches across the center console and encloses my hand in his. His hand is warm and steady as he squeezes my fingers. "I'm so very sorry," he whispers, ducking his head.

"Me too." I squeeze his fingers right back. "It looks like the coast is clear. Shall we?"

Starling grins at my eager expression. "We shall." He pulls a baseball cap low over his face.

In a fluid motion, we step out of the car and amble across the lawn, holding hands like two teenagers in love. Our feet slide into step as we circumnavigate the glass and concrete buildings, keeping our faces down.

Starling leans over and whispers in my ear. "Guard at two o'clock."

My eyes flit in that direction, taking in the scene.

Sure enough, the security guy, dressed all in crisp black and wearing a tool belt, is eyeing us casually, hand on his radio.

I giggle, pretending to whisper something sweet into Starling's ear. "Act casual. If we pretend we belong here, he won't bother us."

My pulse increases as we come even with him, hoping he won't stop us. I have an excuse ready, but I'd rather not have to use it.

Starling reaches up to run a hand through his hair, and then lets his arm drop to swing at his side. His other hand squeezes mine.

We breeze past the guard, who relaxes against the wall, hand dropping from his radio.

I let out a low exhale. That was close.

"We're almost to the memorial garden," I whisper.

"I see you," Haru says. I can't hear its buzz, like a swarm of angry bees, but the surveillance drone she's using to track our progress must be somewhere in the brilliant blue sky.

We round the corner and there it is: the memorial garden. A pond sits off to one side, its surface a chorus of small ripples. Large orange and white Koi fish glimmer under the surface, darting between the water plants and pushing up between the water lilies. Spots of green along the sprawling branches of the trees are the first signs that spring is coming. The sparse trees don't provide much cover, so we'll have to be quick.

I lift my eyes, pretending to gawp at the bright blue sky while noting the positions of the cameras. There's one facing the path that would have caught us approaching the garden, but we'll be long gone before they realize something's happened and comb through their security footage.

Another camera faces the other direction, but we're in luck: there aren't any cameras pointed at the corner of the garden, where there's a large, green utility box tucked against the wall. It saves us time, since we won't have to disable any cameras.

I slip past the pond and under the naked, craggy trunks of the trees.

Starling follows, his head moving back and forth as he keeps an eye on the perimeter. We can't afford to get caught during this first phase of our plan. Being clocked by CIA security would expose us and ruin the exercise we've spent more than a week planning. And we can't waste any time. The longer it takes us to find and plug holes in the CIA's security protocols, the more chances Nexus has to procure the NOC list and agent files himself, and there's no way to know what he'll do with them if he succeeds.

"We're clear," Starling says.

I cut across the grass on a direct path toward the electrical box. There's a simple padlock on the door, and it doesn't take me long to pick it with a couple of slender tools from my clutch purse. The heavy metal door squeals as I open it, the sound much louder than I'd hoped.

I freeze in place, my heart pounding.

If the guard around the corner heard that sound…

A second passes in silence before I spring into action.

Unzipping the inner pouch in my purse, I retrieve the small electrical device that Haru gave me. "I'm inside the panel. What do I do now?"

Haru instructs me through the installation of the device, firing off one command after another. My fingers move over the cables and switches with what I hope is expert precision. I have to install the device correctly, or our plan goes up in smoke.

"Loveday," Starling warns, voice low. "Someone's coming."

A curse slithers past my lips as my fingers plug in the device and I bury it under a couple of long cables inside the box.

"Hurry."

My fingers fly to make the last connection, and I ease the metal door shut.

The sound of jangling keys is sharp in my ears as the security guard closes in on the corner of the building. It's the only thing currently hiding us from view.

There isn't time to lock the box as the guard steps around the corner.

Starling pushes me to one side of the box, tucking me against the wall beside it with strong hands. Leaning forward, he puts one hand on either side of me and moves toward me. His hot breath tickles my ear.

My heart is pounding, and not just because of the security guard who's marching over the sidewalk toward us. "Get away from there!" he shouts.

In my peripheral vision, I can see the padlock hanging open. If the security guard sees it, we're in deep trouble.

I pretend to jump out of my skin, spinning Starling around and ducking behind him.

He gives a sheepish smile. "Sorry, officer. We got a bit carried away."

The guard, whose badge reads Officer Dale, halts three feet away from us. "Get carried away somewhere else, will you? This is an electrical box. It's not safe for you kids to be around."

I will him to remain focused on Starling and me. Don't look at the lock. Don't look at the lock. Don't look...

Dale's attention falters. He's about to glance at the electrical box.

My fingers dig into Starling's arm, and my eyes widen. We're cooked.

Starling waves a hand to catch the guard's attention. "I was wondering, can you explain the significance of the sculpture in the courtyard? It caught my eye earlier. Does it have something to do with codebreaking? I've always been interested in puzzles, myself, mostly crosswords." Starling gives an embarrassed laugh at his rambling.

The guard's eyes move back to us, his face relaxing.

He must not have seen the open padlock.

My insides uncoil in relief when Dale breaks into a grin. "You noticed that, huh? It's pretty cool. It's a sculpture called Kryptos. It's actually got secret messages on it, and me and some of the other guys have been trying to figure them out. We're pretty sure we're getting close. Want to come see?"

"I'd love to." Starling grins eagerly, moving slightly to block me from Dale's view.

Dale turns to lead us away, and it's all the opening I need to click the padlock into place.

Chapter 21

"Happy birthday!" Clarity yells as she throws her body on top of mine.

I groan as I'm abruptly ejected from sleep. "Get off me."

My sister ignores this, instead sprawling over me so that the only body parts I can move are my wriggling toes.

"No air… can't breathe…" I feign choking, which makes Clarity bust up laughing.

"All right," she says, pushing off the mattress and scooting against the wall so I can flip onto my back and sit up in bed. I pull at my black camisole, making sure it's covering my private bits, and focus my eyes on my sister. "What's with the early morning wake-up call?"

"You're eighteen today! And we wanted to make you breakfast."

"Who's we?" I blink rapidly, trying to focus on her.

"Starling, Julep, and me."

"I helped," Lotus says from the doorway.

I whip around to look, and all four of them are standing there, watching Clarity and me. Julep is studiously inspecting her impeccable finger nails, probably in an attempt to give me some semblance of privacy, since I'm still in my pajamas. Lotus and Haru give me cheesy thumbs up. Last, my eyes land on Starling, who is trying not to gape at me and failing miserably.

Alarmed, I pull my quilt up to my shoulders. "Have you been there the whole time?"

Julep smiles without looking up. "Yes, we have."

"Great."

"Now get out of bed," Clarity says, smacking my leg with one hand. "Your breakfast feast is ready, and we're all starving."

Now that she's mentioned food, my senses flicker to life. The aromatic scent of melting butter wafts down the hallway. I imagine the sizzle of it hitting a hot pan.

"Breakfast feast, huh?"

"Yep."

"I could eat a breakfast feast."

"Thought so." Clarity hops off the bed and leads the rest of my team down the hall, leaving the bedroom door agape.

"Shut the door!" I yell after them, but get no response. It looks like I'm going to have to risk jumping down in my camisole and underwear to close it myself. Craning my neck, I listen. Silence. The coast must be clear. I pull my legs up into a crouch, and jump down from my lofted bed. Standing, I stretch my arms. My mouth widens in a yawn.

"I forgot to ask if you—" Starling freezes in the doorway, eyes glued to my bare legs. A blush creeps up his neck.

"Get out!" I shriek, hunching down to cover as much of me as possible.

"I'm so sorry," Starling gushes as he spins away from me, facing the hallway. Even though his back is to me, he's got a hand over his eyes.

My entire body heats in embarrassment as I scramble to pull a pair of pants and a sweatshirt out of my dresser. My heart is pounding a bass rhythm in my chest. Starling just saw me practically naked. It's the epitome of awkward. I can't believe Clarity left our door open like that. When I get my hands on her…

"You look gorgeous, by the way," Starling whispers, so quiet I barely catch it.

My eyes flick to his back, traveling from his neatly trimmed hair to his clean, snug khaki tee shirt to his slim fit jeans and black-socked feet. He doesn't look so bad either, but I keep that thought to myself. "Thanks," I whisper, stuffing down my discomfort and throwing on some clothes.

Once I'm dressed, we stroll down the hallway side by side. Neither of us speaks. Goosebumps rise on my arms at the warmth radiating from him. We aren't touching, but my nerves are humming at how very close we are. If I moved my pinky a hairsbreadth, I could take his hand.

I don't. But I want to.

The sounds of happy chatter and clanging plates get louder as we descend the stairs to the kitchen.

My eyes almost pop out of my head when I catch sight of the table. One large plate is piled high with crisp, golden brown waffles. Bowls of blackberries and raspberries flank them, and there are jars of crystalline maple syrup and peanut butter on the table as well. Hot bacon gleams on another plate, abutted by crisp link sausage.

"Wow, you guys, this looks amazing. Thank you."

Flitting over to me, Clarity gives me a big squeeze. "Happy birthday, sis."

"Happy birthday!" Haru chirps, throwing her arms wide.

"Should we sing?" Lotus asks. "I think so."

And they do. It's the most hideous song I've ever heard in my life, seeing as how neither Lotus nor Clarity can sing on key.

Julep and Haru are better at carrying a tune, but they can't save the savage rendition of "Happy birthday" that assaults my ears. Starling mouths the words, but I'm pretty sure there's no sound coming out.

"How come you're not singing?" Lotus asks, elbowing him.

"You can't make it any worse," I tease.

Starling shakes his head. "Oh yes I can."

It's so bad, there's no way to react except to laugh. So I do. And once my friends are done singing, they burst out laughing too.

"So, singing is not our strong suit," Julep says.

"That was so bad, it was almost prank-worthy," I quip.

"Naw." Lotus smirks. "This definitely doesn't count."

Hopping into a chair, Haru beams. "Let's eat!"

We follow suit, and soon the only sounds in the kitchen are the scraping of forks and little moans of pleasure.

A last minute call takes Royal from the Ivory Tower and effectively postpones my birthday dinner until tomorrow. It doesn't bother me, since it's not the first time it's happened, by a long shot.

Clarity heats up a couple frozen pizzas and sweet talks everyone into playing a game of Ticket to Ride in the den. She turns her big doe eyes to me. "Are you coming?"

Over her shoulder, Starling gives me an encouraging smile.

"No, I have something else I need to do."

Clarity's nose crinkles, but she simply nods. "See you in a bit?"

"Yeah. I'll be back in a couple hours."

She takes my hand and gives it a squeeze before skipping

off to the den with Starling in tow. He glances over his shoulder at me, a question in his eyes, but I wave him off. I'm fine. Really.

With purposeful steps, I enter the parking garage, the keys to Lotus's motorcycle clutched in my hand. In the corner, one of the orange lights is flickering, which casts an eerie vibe over the scene. My instincts are on high alert, but I relax once I'm on the bike with the helmet strapped on, the engine revving beneath me. I'm not sure if I'm getting paranoid, or if the knowledge that Royal would not approve of my little outing is finally getting to me.

It's only a twenty minute drive, but I make it last as long as possible by driving right at the speed limit. More than one person zooms past me, honking in indignation as I slow my motorcycle to a crawl. I'm not sure what I'll find once I get to Bethesda, and the unknown fills me with dread.

I exit the freeway and navigate along the streets into a quiet, old residential neighborhood. Here, the narrow streets are lined with cars, and light shines from the windows of houses wrapped in shiplap with contrasting shutters. My bike moves fluidly through the pools of light created by the yellow glow of the street lights. I'm almost to my destination.

My breathing quickens as I shut off my headlight and continue up the street, hoping to go unnoticed. My grandparents live three houses down from my position. There are no memories of them I can call to the forefront of my mind, since I was a year and a half old the last time I saw them.

Once parked, I scan the street for possible witnesses. The late hour works in my favor. There aren't any pedestrians around that I can see. Slipping off the motorcycle, I stow the helmet before turning toward the one-story brick cottage two houses up the street. A lantern over the porch glows like a beacon as I approach, eyeing the arched front door and white trim glowing in the light of the moon.

My fists clench. My fingers ache to knock on their door, but I shove my hands into the pockets of my leather jacket. Royal is right; they're much safer off not thinking about me.

I tiptoe past the door and creep behind the box hedges that line the front of the house. There's just enough room for me to maneuver myself under the window without my clothing getting snagged on the shrubbery.

With a deep breath, I stretch on tippy toes to peek inside. There's a sole floor lamp lit in the far corner of the room, where an elderly woman sits knitting by its light. In the foreground, an old man lays reclined in a leather chair, eyes half closed as a blue glow flickers over his features from a crime procedural on the television.

The hairs on the back of my neck prickle, and I pull my coat collar tighter over my skin.

A car zooms past, making me duck behind the hedge. It's not wise for me to stay here.

Creeping as soundlessly as possible, I move around the side of the house to another small window.

From this angle, my grandmother is much closer, and her features are thrown into sharp detail by the overhead glow of the light. I recognize her pointed chin and rounded nose as my own. My fingers skim over those parts of my face, awed that there's a woman mere feet away from me whose features look like more aged versions of mine. She could have been my beloved grandma if circumstances were different.

For a moment, my eyes are caught on the movement of her knitting needles as they click together, creating a growing mass that cascades down her lap. I force my eyes away from the motion to survey the room. Tonight will be my first and only visit to this house, and I want to remember as much detail as I can.

Behind my grandfather's recliner, there's a large grouping of picture frames on the wall. Older photos show two little girls in ballet costumes, their cheeks glittering and their shiny hair in precise buns on the tops of their heads. Another picture shows the same two little girls holding hands as they walk along a wooded hiking trail, their hair in long braids down their backs.

My heart leaps into my throat when I catch sight of a small photo off to one side: a young woman, beaming, holding a small baby swaddled in her arms. It's my mom, snuggling a miniature version of me. She was beautiful, and she looks deliriously happy. There's a dull ache in my chest.

I return my gaze to my grandmother and grandfather, but there's no pain in it. These two people are related to me, but I have no emotional ties to them. In another life, they could have been two of my favorite people, but in this one, they're strangers.

After a few minutes, the woman stores her knitting in a wicker basket by her chair. She kisses her husband on the top of his balding head, and disappears into the back of the house. Once his show ends, he turns off the TV and follows. The house goes dark.

It's time to head back to the Tower.

Everyone is preparing for bed by the time I get home. It's a good thing they're not yet asleep, because the loud bump of the music spewing from the security speakers would be enough to waken the dead.

A frustrated groan emanates from Royal's room, but he doesn't emerge. I imagine him shoving his pillow down over his ears, trying to block out the sound. The music fades as I enter the room I share with my sister.

She's just crawling into bed, her face mask perched on her brow, when I crouch down and wrap my arms around her.

"What's this for?"

"Thanks for being the best sister ever.

Clarity pats my shoulder. "You're welcome. Now be quiet so I can go to sleep."

I comply, wondering what on earth is wrong with our security system.

Chapter 22

For once, Clarity is already awake when I rouse the next morning. She's sitting up in bed, peering at the blank, white wall across from our door. "What do you think about putting a big screen in here and setting it up to do a slideshow of nature photos?" She stares wistfully at the white space, absentmindedly picking at her elbow.

I speak through a yawn. "Getting tired of living underground?"

She frowns, lips pursed. "I miss our old house, with that big climbing tree in the backyard, the piles of fall leaves. The window seat." We say it together, smiling at each other.

She looks down at the covers balled up in her lap. Pushing to a stand, she stretches her arms wide. "I think I'll go for a walk."

"Isn't it early for that?"

Clarity shrugs. "Lotus seems to think the early morning is the perfect time to be outdoors."

"He's nuts."

"Maybe, but still."

"I'll come with. Donuts are sounding pretty good right now."

A low vibration draws my attention to my wrist.

Haru
They've hatched.
Control room, people.
It's go time.

The messages propel me out of bed. "Looks like we'll have to walk later." My limbs feel sluggish. Our outing will have to wait. I run headlong into Lotus, and both of us stumble.

"Whoa, whoa," he says, reaching out with both hands to steady me. "Let's try to avoid injuring you right before an important job, yeah?"

I snicker. "Are you calling a ceasefire?"

He grins. "Only temporarily."

Clarity, Julep, and Starling join us, and we hustle toward the control room en masse.

The shuffling of feet and scrape of chairs must alert Royal to our presence, because his office door opens and he peers out. "What's going on?"

"It's time for phase one of our covert assault on the CIA," I say, hushing my words at Haru's wild hand wave.

Royal's eyes widen, and he starts to speak.

Haru glares, putting one finger over her lips to silence him, and then the rest of us.

He exhales and leans against the wall, waiting to see what we're up to.

A shiver of anticipation courses through me. We're so ready for this. The CIA isn't going to know what hit them.

Haru's phone rings in its place on the desk, and a J-pop song bursts from its tiny speakers. She sits up straight in her chair, shoulders back, serious face on, and answers.

"Presidential Pest Control. How can I help you?"

Royal's face contorts in confusion. "What—?"

"SHH!" Clarity hisses, motioning toward Haru, who's still listening to the caller on the other end of the line.

"Cockroaches? How many of them? … Oh dear, that's a lot. … Yes, we can definitely assist you with that. … Let me see… I have a technician in the area. They can be there in an hour. Will that work for you? Great." She repeats the address out loud as she pretends to write it down. In reality, we all have it memorized, since it's always in the back of our minds. "They'll see you in an hour!" She says cheerfully, and then ends the call.

"Let me get this straight," Royal says, raising a hand. "You're posing as pest control workers to get into the CIA? Two days before our exercise?"

"Yep," Lotus says. "Genius, right?"

Royal's expression is curious when he asks, "How did you know they'd be having a cockroach problem?"

I grin at Clarity, who smiles right back. "I planted them. Think of it as a contingency plan."

"You didn't," Royal says, but his proud smile belies his words. "And you re-routed their phones?"

"Starling and I did it when we were there scouting the other day."

Haru raises her hand, but doesn't wait to be called on to speak. "I had them plant a device that would re-route to my phone if anyone in the building tried to call one of the local pest control companies."

Royal nods in approval. "And what is your objective?"

"To clear out the building, so we can access the server room tomorrow," I say. "CIA headquarters is in desperate need of fumigation, since cockroaches are so hard to get rid of."

149

The confused expression resettles on my dad's face. "But that's a day earlier than planned."

Leaning back in my chair, I cross my arms, not even trying to keep the smug look from my face. "Exactly. They'll never expect it."

"It'll be dangerous. Their security team will be using live ammunition, unlike on exercise day."

My head tilts to the side. "So we'll try to avoid getting shot."

Clarity tenses, her mouth forming a thin line.

A flicker of worry crosses Royal's face, but his mouth remains in a sober line. If he has reservations about our plan, he's not sharing them.

I glance around the table at my crew, all but one of whom are eager to proceed. Pushing away from the table, I stand. "Starling, Clarity, get suited up. You know what to do."

We've planned every step with painstaking attention to detail. And this time, we'll succeed.

Chapter 23

It only takes Starling and Clarity a couple minutes to change into their crisp, new uniforms. They both look convincing as pest control workers in the head-to-toe khaki and baseball caps with a cartoon cockroach on the front.

"Looking sharp," I say as they walk into the den.

"Stop. I'm blushing," Clarity says, batting her eyelashes.

Starling actually starts to swagger, which makes him look super cute. Note to self: figure out more ways to make Starling strut.

Haru and Lotus enter from the control room. "Here are your earbuds," Haru says, handing over the tiny devices. "Loveday and I will be on the line the whole time, if you need anything."

"You're sure you don't need a getaway driver?" Lotus asks. "I'm available."

"We've got it under control," Starling says, patting Clarity on the back. "Right, partner?"

My sister's smile is tight. "Yep. Completely under control."

"At least you'll get to go outside now," I joke, hoping to lighten her mood.

Her expression remains pinched.

I step forward, putting a hand on her shoulder. "You've been doing this like a pro for six years. This job's going to be as smooth as silk. Okay?"

Clarity's smile loosens as she meets my gaze, but her eyes aren't in it.

"You know what you have to do?" I ask, looking between the two of them.

"Yes, ma'am," Starling quips, saluting me. "Shall we?" He extends an elbow, which Clarity takes.

"Let's get this over with."

My insides tug as they leave the Ivory Tower. I know it was my decision to send them instead of going myself, but in this moment something about it doesn't feel right.

Once they're gone, I sigh and follow Haru into the control room.

"I think I'll take a nap," Lotus mumbles, his eyes on the floor. He meanders toward the dormitory, probably in search of Julep.

"Enjoy your nap," I call after him, and then duck into the control room.

Haru is already sitting at her laptop. Two large clocks in the upper right corner of her screen show our local time, and the current time in Kuala Lumpur, where her parents live. There's a small window to the right side that shows a glimpse of their living room. Sure enough, her dad is asleep in his recliner, and her mom is moving about the room in a bathrobe, straightening up before going to bed.

I sit in the rolling chair at the next desk and shove off with my feet, coasting until I reach her. "How're they doing?"

"They seem okay. My dad misses me. He keeps asking when I'm coming home. My mom just keeps asking how school is going."

I nod. "Is it going better? With Truly?"

Haru bites her lip. "I think so. Truly says I'm doing much better."

"Good."

"We're almost there," Clarity says over the comms.

"Proceed."

"We're parking now," Starling says. "We'll be inside in a minute."

Haru and I glance at each other, anxious. This is the moment we find out if our plan will even work.

"We're going in," Clarity breathes. The hint of stress in her voice is not lost on me.

"We're right here if you need us."

There's the sound of a door opening. "After you," Starling says.

Clarity thanks him.

The din of footsteps and low conversations filters into my ears.

"Excuse us," Starling says. "We're from Presidential Pest Control. I believe you're expecting us." His southern accent isn't bad.

There's a beat of silence as keys tap at a keyboard. Maureen, the receptionist hums in concentration.

Surely the appointment is on her calendar.

I take a breath, waiting.

"There it is," Maureen exclaims, her voice lighter now. "I'm glad you're here. Everyone is afraid to use the kitchen, and the little devils have taken over the first floor offices." She shudders.

"If you'll show us the way, we'll see what we can do."

"I'd be happy to. We want this taken care of as soon as possible."

Heels click across the tile floor, and I imagine my teammates passing the wall dotted with stars, each of which represents men and women who have died in service to the CIA. My eyes close, picturing those stars, knowing that one has been added recently. For Vale. At this year's memorial ceremony, his parents would have been presented with a replica of one of the marble stars as a reminder of their son's honorable sacrifice.

My eyes prick at the thought, but I push the urge away.

A security check beeps, and Maureen speaks. "Dale, Cliff, these are the pest control people. They're here to take care of our cockroach problem." She gags over these last words, as if even naming the critters turns her stomach.

"Step this way," one of the officers says.

It's quiet but for an electronic beeping sound. It's probably a metal detector they're using to make sure Starling and Clarity are unarmed.

"You're all clear. Go on in."

"Thank you, gentlemen."

A door opens and closes. More footsteps.

"You can't see them, but they were everywhere when the janitor was here last night. She called me, terrified. Apparently there were hundreds of them."

I smirk. Well done, Clarity.

Drawers open and close.

Starling hems and haws, pretending to inspect the area for signs of the pests. "You said something about a kitchen?"

"Right this way."

I sit back in my chair, pleased. Our plan is working out perfectly.

Forty minutes later, the van doors close and Clarity exhales in relief. "I can't believe they bought it."

"I can," I say. "Nobody likes cockroaches."

Beside me, Haru shudders. "You're right. They're disgusting."

"We're all set for tomorrow," Starling says.

"We'll be there bright and early," I say. "Come on back."

"Certainly." Their car engine starts.

Taking out my ear bud, I hand it to Haru. "It's almost time to get started on my birthday dinner. It's going to be delicious."

Haru gives me a hesitant thumbs up.

"Don't worry. I'm not just making salmon. I've got plans for a vegetarian dish you're going to love."

"Great," she says, but won't meet my eyes.

Entering the den, I glance toward the dormitory, but hear nothing. Lotus and Julep must have stepped out.

But when I get to the kitchen, Julep is sitting at the table knitting, a flush on her cheeks.

"You warm? I can turn down the AC."

"I'm fine," she says, smiling sheepishly.

My eyebrows rise, but I choose not to ask. I really don't want to know.

The fridge door crackles as I open it, and light spills out. I reach deep inside, pushing aside sodas, two different labeled milk jugs (almond for Haru and fat free for Clarity), a bag of large, shiny red grapes, and a box of American cheese slices. "Do you know where the salmon I was going to cook for my birthday dinner tonight went?"

Across the room, Julep "hmmphs" into her knitting.

"Weird."

Haru comes traipsing down the stairs. "Starling and Clarity will be back in a minute."

"Great," I say as I straighten up. "Have you seen my

birthday salmon?"

"N-no, I haven't seen it," Haru stammers, reaching a hand up to fidget with her scrunchie.

Closing the sticky fridge door, I turn. "Are you sure?"

Her cheeks turn a rosy pink. "I'm positive. I don't know where it is," she squeaks. "Sorry." She turns and darts away, mumbling something I don't quite catch.

Julep's eyebrows arch. "I wonder what's gotten into her."

"No idea." I peer up the stairs after her. "That was weird. Maybe she hates the smell of fish?"

Music pumps through the Tower's security system, emanating from the small black speakers mounted in the corner of the ceiling.

I push my coat collar up around my ears, wanting nothing more than to shut out the sound. "Dad's gonna kill me."

"He just might," Julep says, still focused on the yarn and needles in her hands.

"Loveday!" Lotus roars as his feet slam on the stairs. He appears at the bottom, arms akimbo. "My car won't start. Do you happen to know where my spark plugs went?"

"Huh," I deadpan. "It's not like them to just walk away."

Lotus glowers at me. "I'm supposed to be driving my route to see how long it will take. I do not want to find out what Royal will do if he finds me here. What did you do with my spark plugs?"

I smirk. "Oh how the tables have turned. And by the way, you are so helping me replace the carpet in the hallway."

His eyes narrow. "Deal. Now tell me where they are."

"Go into the left-side bathroom. Open the toilet tank."

Lotus's hand flies to his mouth to stifle a gag.

"Your precious spark plugs are in a plastic bag, taped to the lid. They should be mostly clean. Mostly."

Lotus grimaces, but there's a hint of awe in his eyes. "That's disgusting." He turns to go, but hesitates on the bottom step. "You may have won this battle." He starts up the staircase.

I yell after him. "I'm winning this war!"

At the table, Julep's eyes gleam. "You two sure are torturing each other. When do you think it'll stop?"

I shrug. "Whenever he admits defeat."

Her brassy laugh fills the kitchen. "Then it's going to be awhile."

"Maybe." I open the fridge again, scanning the shelves even though I know my salmon isn't in there.

"Weird."

"Maybe your dad will agree to take you out for a birthday dinner."

I grin. "I like the way you think." And I leap up the stairs to see if her hypothesis is true.

Chapter 24

For my birthday dinner, Clarity suggested we all dress up. "It'll be so fun," she squealed.

"Oh, I like that idea," Haru added, pretending to hold out a wide skirt and twirl.

Royal listed his head to one side, looking at me for a reaction.

I shrugged. "Sure."

So that's how I now find myself wearing a knee-length, sparkly black dress and a matching black headband. I slip my feet into my only pair of fancy shoes: black kitten heels with tiny bows on the toes. I give myself the once over in the mirror, satisfied with how I look. Clarity's right. It is kind of fun to dress up once in a while. Peering out into the hall to make sure everyone else is busy getting ready, I allow myself a single twirl in Clarity's full-length mirror.

A satisfied smile covers my face.

Starling clears his throat from the doorway, and I whirl to face him, still smiling. He looks really good. His light brown skin glows against his pale gray suit and vivid blue button-up shirt. The top button is undone, exposing the hollow at the base of his throat.

I gulp.

"You look beautiful," he says, eyes flickering from my dress to my hair before resting on my face.

"That's two compliments in two days. You sure know how to spoil a girl."

"I try." The seriousness of his tone makes my heart pound.

"Loveday," he whispers, taking a step toward me. "I wonder if I could ask you a question."

"Yes?" I creep toward him, pulled by an irresistible magnetic force.

"Once we've finished with our operation at the CIA, I'd like to take you out."

"On a date?"

"Yes."

"Like normal teenagers?"

"I've heard they do go on dates, yes."

"Where would we go?"

"A little bird told me you might like to see the new Captain America movie that's coming out soon."

Without realizing it, we've drawn so close to each other that we're mere inches apart. If I wanted, I could stand on tiptoes and kiss Starling's soft, pink lips. My heart leaps into my throat.

"I would like that," I whisper, eyes falling to the lapels of his jacket.

"Hey," he asks, lifting my chin with a gentle finger. "Is there something wrong?"

I bite my lip. "Can I ask you a question first?"

"Anything."

Even though I'm afraid to crack the moment we're having, I have to know. When I speak it's barely audible. "Why didn't you tell me Charles Darnay was your dad?"

Starling sighs as his shoulders sag. "I was afraid that would be it." But he doesn't retreat. His eyes don't waver from mine. He swallows and I notice his Adam's apple bob. Then he answers. "My dad was famous at the Academy. We studied his ops in my classes. Everyone knew I was the son of Charles Darnay and they expected me to be exactly like him. They expected me to be brilliant at everything, and if I didn't measure up they were relentless. I got so tired of being compared to my father all the time. When Royal brought me here, I expected more of the same, but I realized immediately that none of you knew who I was, who my father was, and I can't tell you what huge relief I felt. For the first time in my life, I could be myself without all of the expectations. I wanted to fit here, with your team, as myself, not as the son of a former master spy." Slowly, he reaches out with both hands and wraps his long fingers around my wrists. "I like to think I've succeeded at finding a place here among you. Have I?"

I nod, too dumbstruck by the fizzing sensation in my arms to make an audible response.

"Loveday." It's barely a whisper. Then he's leaning down.

My eyes flutter closed.

Starling presses a light kiss to my lips. "They're waiting for us," he breathes against my skin.

"We can't disappoint them."

"No." His hands drop to mine, giving them a light squeeze before letting go.

My hands feel cold without his touch.

The air is clear and crisp as we walk in a clump toward the restaurant I've chosen: dim sum. It's been too long since I had xiao long bao, and my stomach is rumbling.

Pedestrians stream down the sidewalk, bundled to their ears in thick coats, scarves, and some are even wearing ear muffs, which I thought were only made for toddlers.

Ahead of us, Royal tromps down the sidewalk, his long strides eating the ground under him. The collar of his camel-colored wool coat guards his neck against the frigid air, and his hands are hidden in his jacket pockets.

I glance behind toward Lotus and Julep, who are strolling hand in hand along the curb, daring to make a public display of affection even though Royal could look back and see them at any time.

Lotus catches my eye and smiles, pointing toward their hands and giving me a thumbs up.

I return the gesture with an uneasy smile.

Julep must catch it, because her step hitches for a moment. She falters into step with Lotus, who leans over to whisper something in her ear. Whatever he says brings the smile back to her lips.

A chill wind whips between the buildings, catching the hem of my trench coat and flipping it upward. The resulting shiver wracks my entire body, making me huddle closer to Clarity, who's gliding along at my side. "It's freezing out here!" My teeth chatter.

"You're the one who wanted to walk," she bites back, clutching the lapels of her olive green pea coat with ivory-gloved hands.

"Utter stupidity."

Clarity titters at this.

"What's utter stupidity?" Starling asks, poking his head over my shoulder.

"Me deciding I wanted to walk from the hotel to Chinatown."

"It's a beautiful night. Why not enjoy it?" He grins, wedging himself between us and slinging an arm over each of our shoulders.

I welcome the extra heat and snuggle into his side. My arm snakes around his waist, careful not to poke Clarity. He smells of cedar and peppermint, which only makes me want to press closer to him.

"Better?" he asks.

"Infinitely."

I'm rewarded with a pleased chuckle.

We approach the Friendship Arch—a great green, red, and gold edifice with a tiled, arched roofline that greets visitors to Chinatown.

"Whoa, that's something," Starling says, stopping to gaze upward at the structure.

"It's beautiful," Clarity says, cocking her head to one side.

"Yeah, it's pretty cool," I say, "but let's keep going, okay? I'm freezing out here."

Starling shakes off his reverie and catches up to me, again throwing his arm around me. Leaning down, he whispers, "I'll keep you warm." His hot breath tickles my ear.

I can't stop the blush that rises, so I don't even try.

Clarity skips past us to catch up with Royal and threads her arm through his elbow.

He looks down at her with a gentle smile, and they lead the rest of us along the street to the restaurant.

When we approach, there's someone outside the restaurant waiting. A woman of average height wearing a black coat, dark jeans, and knee-high black leather boots. Her blonde hair floats about her in the light evening wind.

Royal calls out and she turns.

It's Truly.

Chapter 25

My eyes widen in surprise. My dad invited Truly? I mean, I like her and all, but he's never included her in our birthday celebrations before.

As we draw closer, it's apparent that Truly is nervous to see us. Her cheeks are rosy red, and not from the cold. She meets Royal's gaze, and then looks away, embarrassed. The way she's clutching her purse in front of her confirms it.

Clarity turns to meet my eyes. "Told you," she mouths.

Royal pats Truly on the shoulder, smiling widely himself.

"Dog my cats," I whisper.

"What?" Starling asks, laughter in his voice. "Dog my…?"

"Cats. It's an expression of surprise. I didn't know he was inviting Truly."

Starling's eyes scan up the sidewalk to where Royal, Truly, and Clarity are chatting away under the restaurant's green arched eaves. "You didn't know she was coming."

I shake my head. "Nope."

"Are you disappointed?"

"No." As soon as I say it, I know it's true. It feels right, somehow, to have Truly with us. And from the way Royal is looking at her, the way he's hovering, she may be around more often in the future. Clarity was right; our dad likes Truly.

Starling gives my arm a squeeze. "Then let's go say hello."

We close the distance quickly, eager to get inside out of the cold.

Truly beams when she sees me. "Happy birthday!" She throws her arms around me in a hug. "Is it okay that I'm here?" she whispers into my ear.

I answer with a smile. "It's great to see you. I'm glad you're here."

Truly's flush deepens at this.

"Let's all go inside, shall we?" Royal asks, glancing up the sidewalk to where Lotus and Julep are hustling toward us, no longer holding hands. "It's chilly out here." He holds the door open and ushers us inside. The restaurant's customers hunch further down in their seats when the cold gust from the open door hits them, so Royal snaps the door closed. "Brr," he says, pretending to tremble. He's being downright… cheesy. Truly must bring it out of him, because up until now I'd never describe my dad as silly.

Inside, the restaurant is lit by warm white globe sconces that illuminate the whimsical tapestries on the walls. The tables are crowded with people, and servers whisk shining metal carts around the room, stamping patrons' orders with rubber stamps and leaving behind steaming baskets of delicious bite-sized goodness. The warm scents of pork, ginger, and garlic permeate the air, making my stomach growl in anticipation.

A short, older man with wrinkled brown skin and a white goatee smiles at the sight of us and moves through the overflowing tables toward us, dodging food carts with practiced ease. "Royal! So good to see you." He extends a hand and shakes with my dad.

"Zhang Wei! We're happy to be here. I brought six hungry

164

people with me."

"That's what I like to hear," the man says, nodding once. "Allow me to show you to your table. It's the best in the house." He leads us toward the back of the restaurant to a large table draped with a pristine white tablecloth. "Right next to the kitchen. You'll have your pick of the food."

"Thank you," Royal says.

Zhang Wei nods again before melting into the crowd.

My dad gestures for us to be seated. I scoot onto the bench against the wall, followed by Clarity. Truly slides in beside her, and Royal sits at the head of the table. He scoops up the ordering form and scans it. Starling sits across from Royal, and Julep and Lotus take the chairs facing Clarity and me. Immediately Lotus twists in his seat to scan the food carts. He must see something he wants, because he swipes the order form from Royal and bolts out of his seat across the restaurant.

I can't help but laugh into my hand. "Someone's hungry."

"I think he's got the right idea," Starling says, eyeing a neighboring table's plates hungrily.

The kitchen door swings open and a server emerges, pulling a cart behind him. The man doesn't get more than three feet into the room before Royal waves him over and selects a bunch of items for us to share.

My mouth waters at all of the yummy foods laid out before us on the table. Reaching out, I I'm in the middle of taking one of each when Lotus jogs toward us, holding another food tray in his hand. "Anyone want a fried sesame bun?" he asks as he slides into his chair.

"Aren't those a dessert?" Julep asks, reaching for one.

"That's what's so great about dim sum," Lotus explains. "There's no correct order to eat things in." He snaps a couple photos with his phone before digging in.

165

"Agreed," I say, taking an entire basket of shrimp dumplings.

Starling extends a hand toward them, but I swat him away with my chopsticks. "Get your own," I tease.

"Oo, someone's not feeling like sharing," he retorts, amusement in his eyes.

"It's my birthday."

"It certainly is." He flags down a server and gets another basket of shrimp dumplings for the table.

"This all looks so good," Truly says. "Where do I start?"

"You've never had dim sum?" Clarity asks.

"I've never had the chance, but I've always wanted to try it."

"You're in for a treat," Clarity says. She leans toward Truly and gives a whispered explanation of the different dishes dotting our table.

Over their heads, Royal catches my gaze. He gives a slight head tilt toward Truly and raises his eyebrows in question. He's asking me if it's okay that she's here, that he invited her.

Not sure what to do, I give him a thumbs up. It feels awkward, but it does the job.

Royal's shoulders relax and he turns his attention to his food.

During the course of dinner, it becomes obvious to everyone at the table that there is something romantic going on between Truly and my dad. They spend a fair bit of time talking in low voices with each other, him smiling and relaxed and her flushed and happy.

Clarity sends a handful of significant looks my way, and I finally wave her off with a mouthed, "Yes I see."

Her eyes rest on Truly and my dad once more, a pleased smile on her lips.

For my part, I'm not sure how I feel about the whole thing. I like Truly, a lot, but it's weird seeing my dad act like a guy paying attention to a pretty woman. For all of our lives, it's just been Dad, Clarity, and me. As far as I know, the only women he's ever been involved with were my mom and Clarity's. But the way he looks at Truly makes it clear that he's enchanted by her. No joke, he even pulls the yawn and stretch at one point, which makes Truly smile so wide it looks like her face is going to split in half.

My mind starts to wander. How will this work if it gets serious? Would Truly move into the Tower with us? Would she continue working as a teacher, or would she quit to maintain a lower profile, as part of our family? I bite my lip, thinking over the possibilities.

"Earth to Loveday." Lotus leans over the table to wave a hand in my face.

My instincts kick in. I snatch it out of the air, bending his fingers back before I realize I'm about to break them. Eyes wide, I release his hand.

He sits back in his chair, wiggling his fingers to make sure they're all still intact. "Somebody's wound a little tight," he says.

"Sorry, I was somewhere else."

"Clearly."

"Are you worried about tomorrow?" Royal asks, sliding his arm out from behind Truly's shoulders and leaning toward me.

I shake my head. "No. Maybe. It's a big deal." I smile at Royal. "I'm fine. We're ready."

His focus lingers on me for a moment, and then he relaxes

against the chair. "I'll take your word for it."

"Anyway…" Lotus says. "Is it time for presents?" He pulls out a small plastic pouch and tosses it to me. "I didn't wrap it."

Nose crinkled, I turn it over. "Gross." I toss it back.

"What? You don't like bacon and cheese flavored crickets?"

I grimace. "No thanks."

"Are those real?" Truly asks. "May I see them?"

Lotus hands her the foil packet.

She takes them in one hand and flips over the package so she can read the back. "They're real," she murmurs in surprise. "I wonder what they taste like." Glancing up, she realizes there are six pairs of eyes on her. She rips open the package without hesitation. "Who wants to try one?"

I shake my head. "You go ahead."

"I'll take one," Lotus says.

"You would."

He smirks at me.

"I'll have one as well," Starling says. At the sight of my wide eyes, he says, "Growing boys need to eat, and all that."

"Indeed."

"I'll have one too," Haru puts in, jiggling in her seat. "I've tried them fried before. They're actually pretty good."

Beside me, Clarity declines.

Truly hands out the flavor-coated insects.

"On three?" Truly asks. At the boys' nods, she counts. "One, two, three." She pops hers into her mouth and crunches down on it, chewing slowly.

Lotus and Starling do the same.

"Huh," Lotus says.

"What do they taste like?" I ask.

"Chicken." He grins.

I throw a balled up napkin at him, which he attempts to dodge. It bounces off his shoulder and falls to the ground behind him.

"Anyone else?" Truly asks, holding up the small bag. She doesn't get any takers, so she hands the bag to Lotus, who pockets it.

"Seriously, though, is it time for presents?" Lotus asks, looking around the table at us.

"Definitely," I say.

Clarity gives me tickets to the National Museum of Women in the Arts. "We'll go on a sister date," she says with a smile.

"Perfect. Thanks."

Royal gives me a crisp, white envelope. "Open it."

I do, finding a receipt inside. My eyebrows furrow in question as I look up to meet his eyes.

"It's a receipt for a brand new model handgun, and some ammo. I thought you'd like to try it. It's in my safe in the Tower."

"Thanks, Dad."

He smiles at my use of the endearment, probably glad it's not being followed up by an outlandish request.

Julep gives me a beautiful, knitted black scarf she made herself.

"It's so soft," I say, wrapping it around my neck.

"You're welcome," she says.

Lotus's real gift for me is a staple gun. "For redoing the carpet in the hall," he quips.

Starling slides a slender, neatly wrapped box across the table toward me, a sheepish smile on his lips.

"What is this?" I ask, picking it up and shaking it. There's a hint of movement inside. Some kind of fabric, maybe?

"Did you wrap that?" Lotus asks, shooting an incredulous look at Starling.

"Are you insinuating that because I'm male, I can't gift wrap?"

Lotus nods, lips puckered.

"I can't speak for my entire sex, but in my case, you'd be right. I had it gift wrapped at the shop."

Lotus grins, vindicated.

I peel away the pristinely folded wrapping paper and open the box. Inside, neatly folded, is a pair of beautiful black leather gloves, whisper thin and as soft as velvet. "These are amazing," I breathe, sliding them onto my hands. They fit perfectly, like they were made for my fingers. "Thank you."

Starling's eyes twinkle as I meet his gaze. "You're welcome."

"They'll come in handy, tomorrow, I'm sure," Clarity says, taking my hand and admiring the meticulous seams.

I'm balling up the wrapping paper and tucking it into the plastic bag one of the servers provided when Truly lifts a small, neatly wrapped box out of her purse. "I got you a little something too," she says, holding it out to me.

I take it and know in an instant, by its weight and size, that Truly's gift is a book. Peeling away the wrapping paper, I discover a vintage copy of *The Phantom Tollbooth*. It's bound in worn black leather with a gold image of a little boy and a clockwork dog on the cover.

"It was my favorite as a little girl," she explains. "And Royal told me you're fond of classic children's books."

I run a finger over the golden image, knowing it'll look great beside the vintage books of my mothers' that I keep in my desk drawer. It's an incredibly thoughtful gift. "It's beautiful," I say at last. "Thank you."

Truly's smile relaxes. Under the table, Royal pats her knee. And doesn't remove his hand.

I force my eyes down to the bits of food on my plate, snatching up the last egg tart and taking a large bite to give myself something to do. Watching my dad put a hand on Truly's knee is weird. Not bad, but weird.

Chapter 26

The city lights bounce off the cloudy sky, making it appear a hazy canopy of steel gray in the hours before dawn. Inwardly, I run through the plan again, looking for holes. There are some definite risks, but I think it'll work. Lotus, Clarity, Haru, Starling, and I are about to stage our second covert assault of CIA headquarters. And this time we're going to succeed.

Lotus steers up the parkway, easing around corners at a crawl to compensate for the fact that he's driving with his headlights off. "You ready?" he takes a quick glance at me before his eyes return to the road. His fingers grip the steering wheel at nine and three.

I inhale deeply, looking at the road ahead. It's empty, as it should be at 04:00. "Yep."

"You have some snacks in case you get hungry in there?"

One side of my mouth lifts. "I swiped a couple of Clarity's protein bars. They should do the trick."

"And bug repellent? Gloves?"

"In my belt." I point to where it's situated on the floor at my feet.

"All right. Here we are." He pulls to the side of the road, and the wheels crunch over fallen sticks and leaves.

I meet his eyes. "See you when this is over."

He winks.

"Here I go." I pull my black balaclava over my head and open the car door. With steady legs I push out into the night, fastening my utility belt around my waist as I move into the treeline. From here on in, stealth will be key. My shoes crunch the brittle detritus that litters the ground. A flicker of doubt lights in my belly. Maybe I should have had Clarity do this part. She is, after all, practically a ghost when she moves. No. I couldn't do that to my sister. Her recent hesitance to work in the field would have been a liability tonight, when we can't afford to make any mistakes. I steel myself and press forward. I can do this easily. It'll be just like the night months ago when I broke into Cobalt Security. Even the tools are the same.

Around me, night sounds fill the air. Crickets chirp. Owls hoot. Some type of rodent squeaks in fear. I take another step and the chirping stops abruptly. It's eerie how they do that, only starting up again once I move past them.

I reach the road that circumnavigates the agency grounds. Here I go. My pulse speeds.

I scan up and down the road, but there's no sign of movement. Using a burst of energy, I leap across the road and freeze, listening for any nearby security personnel.

All is quiet.

"I'm across the road. Proceeding to phase two."

"Go ahead," Haru answers over the comms.

In a silent motion, I retrieve my gloves from my belt and slide them over my hands. They'll protect my palms from being injured and eliminate the need to worry about leaving fingerprints.

Kneeling down, I prostrate myself on the ground. From here on in, I army crawl.

173

The lights and cameras around the building are motion activated, but I'm betting they don't light up when small animals such as raccoons or possums mosey over the grass. It's a risk, but I have to take it.

The night grass is slick with moisture that seeps into my clothing and chills my skin. Still, I press forward. I'm almost to shelter. The corner of the building is edged by shrubberies that will hide my presence should a security guard walk past.

"There's a guard twenty yards away," Haru whispers into my earbud. "Get to cover as fast as you can without making any noise."

Cold sweat breaks out on my skin. I put on a burst of speed and slither over the grass like an angry cobra. The shrubs are ten feet in front of me.

Five.

Two.

I turn onto my back and shimmy under the bush, ignoring the tiny twigs that pull at my knit balaclava.

Footsteps approach along the pathway.

The crackle of a radio sounds around the building. The guard is close.

I tuck my feet under me, praying whoever it was didn't see me.

"He's almost on top of you." Haru's voice is a squeak of worry.

A security light comes on, throwing bright white light over the walkway and the surrounding grass, mere inches from where I'm hidden.

I don't move.

"Shh, I'm listening," Haru hisses at someone on the other end of the line.

My breaths are shallow, undetectable, as the security guard

rounds the corner and stops, peering across the lawn. He plucks his radio from his belt and speaks into it. "There's nothing here. Must have been a raccoon or some other critter Jensen saw on the camera."

"All black?" the response comes. "Maybe a skunk."

The security guard tenses at this.

"Don't worry, Murphy. Jones has some of his organic tomato juice in the fridge if you get sprayed." The man's laughter filters through the radio.

Murphy scowls down at the device in his hand.

"Check the area, and then come on back."

"Roger," Murphy says. He shifts on his feet, taking gingery steps, probably in an attempt to avoid spooking whatever creature he thinks is out here. I don't blame him; I wouldn't want to encounter a skunk either. Hopefully his reticence will work in my favor.

But I'm not so lucky.

Murphy holsters the radio, pulls his flashlight out of his belt, and shoots the beam right at me before I have a chance to move.

I'm frozen to the ground.

The guard's eyes widen. "Don't move," he commands. His hand slips toward his gun. I can't let him reach it.

Like lightning, my own hand moves to my belt, taking out my tranquilizer gun and firing one shot as Murphy throws up a hand to protect himself.

The tiny dart embeds itself in his forearm. His mouth forms an aghast O as he looks from me to his arm.

Then he crumples to the sidewalk in a heap.

So much for the element of surprise.

The hairs on the back of my neck stand up as the man's radio crackles. "Murphy, you found that skunk yet?" A pause.

175

"Murphy?"

Above me, the security light goes out.

My mind scrambles for purchase. They'll be sending backup in moments.

I move to a crouch, listening for the sound of approaching footsteps. I'll have to make this quick. As fast as I can, I crawl out of my hiding place and snatch the dart from Murphy's arm. Then, I whirl around to face the building, scanning for my target entry point.

There it is.

A few yards away from me there's a large vent mounted to the side of the building, a few inches from the ground. "I'm going in," I whisper, just loud enough for Haru to hear me.

"Thank goodness you're okay," she says, and then checks herself. "Proceed."

Careful to move on the outside edges of my feet and hands so I don't leave prints, I advance toward the vent. In a few seconds, I've removed three screws and loosened the last one enough that I can swivel the vent cover to one side and push myself inside. It's a tight squeeze, like I knew it would be. The icy metal of the duct cuts through my clothes, making me shiver. Pivoting in place as well as I can in the small space, I grip the metal slats of the cover between my fingers and pull it shut as best I can from the inside. I'm counting on them not looking at it too closely in their search of the grounds.

If they do, they'll know I'm already inside the building. It would make my team's job much more complicated, if not impossible.

Several pairs of boots stamp along the cement outside. The light comes on, illuminating three fully tricked-out security guards as they round the corner. They scan the building's wall, the pathway, and the lawn in silence.

The only objects between them and me are the shrubs and the vent cover. Not much.

My heart pounds as they move slowly up the sidewalk toward my hiding place. Their bodies are taut, alert, and their eyes are in a constant state of movement.

I don't dare breathe as they approach.

My heart is pounding so loud I could swear it was echoing off the metal duct around me.

The guards pause right outside my vent. All that's visible of them is their legs from the knees down. If one of them decides to look inside the vent, I won't have any warning.

I'm a sitting duck.

My fingers grip my tranquilizer gun in both hands, holding it at the ready. If they come for me, maybe I'll be able to take down at least one of them first.

Another long moment passes.

The guards push off the pathway and fan out in the grass, moving away from me into the dark beyond the field of light.

My lungs are sore from holding my breath in, but still I wait. A few more seconds.

The air pushes out of my in a whoosh as I part my lips.

Across the grass, the security guards are phantoms rippling through the dark.

I've made it inside the CIA undetected, mostly. Now all I have to do is get in position.

Turning around in the duct, I grope with my hands to get an idea of the direction it takes into the building. Haru's plans were right. Shimmying on my stomach, I push further inside.

Me
I made it to the store, just before closing.

Haru

177

I'm glad you made it.
There are so many people out walking their dogs tonight!
The park is full of them.

Me

One of them's already been sprayed by a skunk.
Those things are sneaky.

Haru
Lotus says, "I hope you bought tomato juice."

Me

Tell him I have everything I need.

Haru
Okay!
Starling and Clarity are looking forward to hanging out
tomorrow.

Me

Me too.

My body is steady as I creep along the duct, further into the
belly of the building, freezing at any nearby sound. If I'm found
now, sneaking into the CIA outside the time allotted for our
exercise, I'll be in deep trouble, and not even Royal will be able
to shield me from the full force of it.

Chapter 27

My heart pounds in my chest as I listen to the voices echoing through the vents. From what I can tell, and Haru has confirmed it, there are still a number of security personnel sweeping the grounds to find the trespasser. Once Murphy came to, about fifteen minutes ago, he told them he'd seen a kid in the flowerbed, and then he'd fainted. Miraculously, he didn't remember being shot with a tranquilizer gun, and he didn't have any idea if the kid he'd seen was a boy or a girl. One of the advantages of being small and flat chested. I'm harder to ID.

From my memory of the building's blueprints and schematics, I'm in one of the vents that leads directly to the basement. The thing about having all of those computer servers is that they have to be kept from getting too warm. Hence all the vents and air ducts.

I'm about to scramble under a grate that leads into one of the rooms on the first floor when the light in the room comes on. Narrow beams filter through the slats of the grate, illuminating my hands.

My eyes widen, and I draw them into the shadows a centimeter at a time to prevent the vent from creaking under my movement.

Footsteps vibrate directly above me.

I count two sets of footfalls. Two CIA security guards. And they're less than a yard away from my hiding place.

"Murphy said he thought it was a kid?" one asks.

"That's what he said."

The two men move into the room, their steps vibrating across the floor.

"And then he fainted?"

"Don't look at me. Maybe he had low blood sugar or something?"

"But Murphy isn't diabetic."

A grunt. "Maybe he skipped his lunch break. You know he's been stressed out, trying to work overtime before the baby comes."

The footsteps stop a few feet away.

If it was possible to make myself any smaller, I would.

"Room's clear. Let's go."

"You got it."

The light in the room goes out, shrouding me once again in darkness.

As they step away, out into what I'm guessing is the hall, one of them radios. "First floor is clear."

So they *are* sweeping the entire building.

I purse my lips, almost wishing I had grabbed Murphy's radio. It would have been a handy way to keep tabs on all of the security officers in and around the building. But I couldn't risk it. Someone may have heard it go off inside the vent, and then I would have been toast.

The footsteps recede to another area of the building, taking their radio with them.

I scurry under the vent grate and make a right. The

basement shouldn't be far now.

My hands slide forward but feel nothing. My arms lurch into the dark, pulling me down. I scramble for a handhold, but my palms swipe at the slick metal. There's nothing to grab hold of, and my body careens downward into the black. I hit the sides of the vent as I fall, bruising my elbows and knees.

I land with a thud in an awkward hand stand, my body upside down in the narrow duct. It's a good thing I'm not claustrophobic, or these tight spaces would be getting to me by now.

I push the thought away. Dwelling on the limited amount of space I have to maneuver is not a smart thing to do at the moment. Taking a deep breath, I fold my arms and force myself through the L-shaped bend in the duct. It leads to another horizontal space. Vent grates on the left of the duct indicate that the basement is on that side.

Pressing my ear against the cold metal, I listen. There's not a sound in the basement, other than the whirr of computer fans. Hopefully that means no-one heard my graceless, noisy fall. The duct here is bigger than the one upstairs, so I can move forward on my hands and knees. Once I reach the first grate, I peer out.

The server room is dark and empty but for the rows of computer towers that line three of the room's walls and march out across the floor, leaving a small open space near the door. Narrow spaces between the banks of servers leave just enough room for the technicians to work on the machines, their lights blinking green and blue. The lone desk and chair near the door are deserted.

A relieved sigh escapes me.

Me
I made it to my friend's house.

181

I think I'll sleep over.

Haru
Good idea.
Night!

I stretch out on my back in the vent, careful to position myself between two of the openings so that, on the off chance someone looks inside the grate, they won't be able to see me. I try to close my eyes, but my brain won't shut up about tomorrow. It's going to be a long night.

My stomach growls, but I lie still, listening.

There's still no sound in the basement of the building, so either their security has already swept down here, or they're not here yet. Either way, I have an opportunity. Reaching down to my belt, I open one of the small, magnetic pouches and take out one of Clarity's protein bars. I chew it slowly, hoping it'll be enough to last me until I can get a decent meal tomorrow.

After a time, the sounds of movement in the upper parts of the building recede. Everyone but essential personnel must have given up the search and gone home for the night.

I lay in the dark, eyes closed. At some point, I fall asleep.

Light floods the basement, waking me at once. My instincts are screaming at me to get up and get moving, but I ignore them.

There's a low click, and the door to the basement swings open.

My heart starts to pound. It could be the security personnel finally getting around to checking the basement. If I make a sound, what's to stop them from shooting first and asking questions later? They aren't expecting us to initiate the exercise until tomorrow, after all. My pits start to sweat. I've thought about dying. In my line of work, who hasn't? But I never expected it to be in an air duct inside CIA headquarters.

A single individual shuffles into the room.

The scent of hot coffee hits my nostrils, making my mouth water.

A chair creaks as the person sits. Fingers clatter over a keyboard.

Inching my watch upward, I check the time. It's only 07:30. My body relaxes. It must be someone who needed to work with the servers before the building is closed for fumigation in a couple hours. I lower my arm to my side. And that's when the duct creaks.

The worker stills. I imagine their wrists poised, fingers hovering over the keyboard.

I freeze, cursing in my head. Hoping against hope that he or she won't think to get someone to check the building's vent system.

I don't dare move. I'm still for so long my muscles start to ache from being held in the same position. Still I remain.

My watch screen lights up, but I don't dare move to read the message, not as long as there's someone in the basement working.

The tiny screen flickers on and off several more times. It's probably Haru, checking up on me, or Starling or Clarity telling me they're on their way.

After a long moment, the typing resumes.

Minutes pass by, and my butt has fallen completely asleep pressed against the vent.

Whoever is in the basement shifts in their seat, and the chair creaks again. They gather their things and leave the room. The door clicks locked behind them.

I exhale in relief.

That was too close.

Slowly, I move to my hands and knees, ignoring the pins and needles as blood flows to my previously snoozing body parts.

Another check of my watch reveals the time to be 08:47. And I have messages from Haru, Starling, Clarity, and Lotus.

Haru
Starling and Clarity are leaving home now.
They'll be there to meet you in about half an hour.

Starling
I hope you slept well.
The first night in a new bed can be rough.

Clarity
See you soon, sis.
P.S. I'm bringing you a whole box of your favorite toaster pastries.

A grin rises to my lips. My sister is the best.

Lotus
Have fun sleeping with the creepy crawlies?

Me
Not a one in sight.

Lotus
Really?
I thought they loved dark, confined spaces.

Me

Don't remind me.

Lotus
winky emoji

I reach up and turn on my earbud. Now that I'm alone in the room, it'll be quicker to communicate this way.

Me
I'm not busy, so call if you need anything.

Haru
Gotcha.

"Good morning!" Clarity chimes through the comms. "Don't respond if it isn't safe, but I thought you might like to hear a friendly voice after your long night."

"Good morning," Starling adds.

"Morning," I whisper.

"There you are," my sister says. "We're heading your way. We'll be there in about fifteen minutes."

"Great."

"Are you ready for this?" Starling asks.

"I am," Clarity says. "If our plan works, everything should be over in two hours."

Two hours. It's not a lot of time, but then our plan is straightforward. Simple. Mostly.

I listen as Starling and Clarity chatter during their drive, more thankful than ever for our earbuds. I don't risk talking much, but it's wonderful feeling my teammates are close by.

"We're pulling into the lot," Starling says finally.

The engine cuts out and two car doors open and close.

"Here we go," Clarity says.

"There are two security personnel standing outside the entrance, and it looks like there are several more inside."

I'm not surprised. After their "kid" sighting last night, I expected them to be doubly cautious today.

"Good morning, officers," Starling says, his voice a model of servitude. "Has everyone been cleared out of the building?"

"It's all clear." I don't recognize the voice. The shifts must have changed while I was asleep.

"All of the windows are shut tight, and all the interior doors are open?"

"Yes, just like you asked."

"Excellent. Then if you don't mind, my partner and I will do a check of the building before we bring in the fans."

"I'll escort you."

"That won't be necessary. We'll be quick."

"I'm under orders."

Starling hesitates. This conversation isn't going how we hoped. "All right then. Let's go."

Starling, Clarity, and the officer enter the building.

I scoot forward just enough to peek out one of the vent grates into the basement.

I listen in silence as they check each floor, making sure all the interior doors are open and all windows are sealed.

"Oops. Missed one," Starling says. A window slides closed. "Good thing we always check first."

The guard grunts in response.

Clarity laughs.

My eyes blink closed in the dark. I have no idea how Starling and Clarity are going to shake their security detail, but they have to so they can let me out of the vent.

After several minutes, I can feel the vibrations as they approach the basement.

Here we go.

"Uh oh, I see a door that's still closed. We'll have to open it," Starling says. The knob on the basement door rattles. My pulse increases.

"No can do. That door stays closed." The man's voice is firm, all business.

"But if we don't fumigate the entire building, the roaches will come right back."

There's a pause. "I'll call and check." The security guard moves away from my teammates to make the call.

We wait in silence, hoping for a favorable response.

My heartbeat booms in my ears.

The guard returns. "If I unlock the door, can you put a bug bomb inside?"

"Sure," Clarity says. "Let me go get one out of the truck." Her footsteps grow quieter as she walks out of the building.

It's a good thing I was prepared for this. Reaching down, I lift up my shirt and retrieve the gas mask that I have strapped to my lower back. Itchy and irritated red lines remain where the straps chafed my skin. I put the mask on over my mouth, nose, and eyes a quietly as I can.

"Here it is," Clarity says as she rejoins the two men outside the server room door. "Once we set this off, everyone is to remain outside this room for at least two hours. Is that okay?"

"That's fine." Two electronic beeps sound. "Go ahead." The knob turns, the lights flicker on, and Clarity steps into the room. Her eyes sweep the area before resting on the vent I'm hiding behind. I could swear she's looking right at me, but that's impossible since she doesn't know exactly where I'm located in the duct.

"I'll just be a minute," Clarity says. "Why don't the two of you finish checking the rest of the building?"

"No. Set the bomb, and then step out. I'm not authorized to leave anyone unattended in this room."

"Important computers, eh?" Starling asks. All I can see of him through the open doorway is his elbow, clothed in the khaki brown of the pest control uniforms we ordered.

I can't see the response he gets, but the silence suggests that the guard does not have a sense of humor.

"Okay," Clarity says, speaking just a bit louder than necessary. "I'm setting the bomb. Once I do, we have to get out quickly. It's not safe to breathe in the chemicals."

The guard moves into the doorway, watching Clarity's every move.

My sister moves the desk chair into the middle of the open area, sets the bug bomb on it, and triggers it. She steps out of the room and the door shuts behind her. Its lock clicks into place.

So much for them letting me out of the vent.

Chapter 28

The bug bomb goes off, sending a spray of chemicals into the air.

I've got to get out of the duct, fast.

My hands make quick work of a zippered pouch on my belt, pulling for a tiny rotary tool. "Always come prepared," Royal says. I'm glad I listened to that particular adage.

"All right, the entire building is clear," Starling says over the comms. "If you'll allow us, we'll get the fans from the van and prep for fumigation."

"By all means."

Footsteps crunch on the ground outside, and the van door slides open.

My breathing goes shallow. I have to hurry. But using the rotary tool is a risk. In the silent basement, the multipurpose tool will be deafening when I turn it on. And if I'm lucky and no one hears it, I still have to contend with the sparks it'll make as it cuts through the vent cover. There's a very real possibility that one of the sparks could shoot out into the room, ignite the chemicals hanging in the air, and make the whole basement explode.

It would eliminate the CIA's security risk, and me with it.

I purse my lips, my fingers tightening around the rotary tool in my land. The only other item I've got in my belt that could get me through the metal vent cover is my laser glass cutter, and it wouldn't be any less flammable than the rotary tool. My eyes catch on the tiny circular blade in my hand.

Here goes everything.

I flip the switch and the blade whines into action.

"Did you hear that?" one of the guards says, his voice filtering through my earbud.

My eyes widen, but I don't shut off the tool. Instead, I press it against the vent grate and get to work. It sparks as it makes contact, making me thankful for my gas mask and thick clothing.

"I don't hear anything," Starling says, his voice casual.

"Hmm."

"Did you hear something?" the man asks again.

"No," another guard responds.

"Sounded like a power tool."

"Someone nearby must be doing some work."

"Yeah…" His voice is hesitant, but the guard drops the subject.

The metal of the grate glows red under the rotary tool, but the gas mask blocks my nose from smelling the burning scent it's putting off.

I'm through the first piece of metal. Only a bunch more to go.

Outside the duct, the bug bomb has carpeted the entire room in a white, foam-like dusting of poison. The servers look like rectangular Christmas trees, flocked white with blinking lights.

The next pieces of the vent cut more quickly, but this is still taking longer than I would like.

Starling grunts. "Due to the size of the building, we'll set up three fans per floor."

"That's a lot of fans."

"It sure is, but we like to be thorough."

"The fans circulate the chemicals, making fumigation much more effective." Clarity shows off the fruit of her time spent researching pest control methods over the past week.

"Sure," the guard says. "I'll take you inside whenever you're ready."

"We're ready."

The doors open, and my teammates step into the building. I've still got three more metal slats to cut.

"Let's do the basement first," Starling says. "We'll work our way up."

It's a warning.

I switch off the tool, my muscles tense in the silence.

The grind of the elevator announces their descent into the basement. I can hear all three of them as they place the fans, and then move into the elevator.

"Next up, first floor," Clarity says.

I wait until they're on the second floor before I fire up the rotary tool again. I can't afford for the security guard to hear me, but I'm running out of time. The plan was to be out of the building by the time Starling and Clarity are ready to begin fumigating, so the security would be focused on them and not the perimeter, but that isn't looking likely now.

I push the rotary tool into the metal slats with all my might, hoping to speed it along.

The last two metal slats split under the tiny spinning wheel, their tips still a burnished red from the heat. I'm through.

Scooting around in the vent, I press my feet against the

metal slats and push. My muscles strain, but slowly they bend outward, jutting into the empty basement. So much for getting in and out without leaving clues as to how I did it.

I flip around again so I'm on my hands and knees, my face just inside the vent opening. With one more deep inhale, I squeeze out of the jagged hole onto the basement floor. In a moment, my gloves are coated in the white dust. It's going to leave handprints on everything I touch, like a connect-the-dots illustration of my time in the basement. Great.

I swipe my gloves on my pants, leaving white streaks up and down the black fabric. It looks like I rolled around in sidewalk chalk, but at last my gloves are sufficiently clean.

Stepping up to the nearest server tower, I scan the machine, looking for a port through which to connect my tablet to the CIA's servers. There it is.

I slip a tablet the size of a deck of cards out of my belt, along with a tiny aux cord, and plug it into the tower. The tablet comes to life as it recognizes the input. A menu appears, requesting a password. This is new, but I'm prepared. I open an app on the tablet. A window pops up, and the app starts trying permutations in rapid succession.

Seconds tick by, and my ears strain to listen to any sound that might hint at danger.

The tablet flashes, notifying me that the password has been found. I'm in.

I scan through the list of folders until I find the ones I'm looking for. Sliding the thumb drive Haru gave me into place, I highlight the files I want.

A download progress bar appears at 3 percent. Four percent. Ten. It continues to climb quicker than the first time. My shoulders sag in relief. It may have taken me longer than expected to get into the server room, but it looks like the "download" is going to go more quickly, helping me make up time.

"That's the last fan," Starling says through the earbud. "The next step is to get the fumigation packs from the van and set them up. It'll only take about five minutes. Then we're ready. It's important to make sure no one goes inside for at least the next 48 hours. Okay?"

"Of course." The guard sounds bored.

I can't help but snicker. He's awfully chill for a guy whose squad member got knocked out by a "kid" with a tranquilizer gun less than twelve hours ago.

A pop-up on my tablet announces that the fake download is complete. I wiggle the cord out of the server port, stow the tablet, cord, and drive in my belt, and climb into the vent.

The van door slides open.

"Are you out?" Clarity whispers.

"Almost," I whisper. "Give me a minute."

Climbing through the vent's vertical leg is a challenge, but I'm able to do it by bracing my back against one side of the metal casing and shuffling my hands and feet upward along the opposite side.

Once I reach the straightaway, I thread through the duct. Sunlight appears up ahead. I'm ten feet from my gateway to open air.

My heartbeats grow louder, drowning out all sound.

I approach the vent cover and peer out. There's no one in sight.

With one hand, I swing the grate upward and slide out on my stomach, lowering the vent cover into place against the side of the building without making a sound. My eyes scan the area around me. There's not a security guard in sight. Perfect. "I'm out."

"Good," Clarity says. "Okay," she continues, louder. "We'll post warning signs at all of the entrances, and then we're ready to start pumping the gas into the building. As my co-worker mentioned, we advise everyone to stay out for at least two full days. At that point, we'll come back and do a check. If everything looks good, we'll open up and air out."

I push my gas mask up my face, leaving it strapped to my head. In a burst of pent-up energy, I sprint over the grass and across the road at top speed, hurtling into the trees.

"Lotus, you in position?" I huff as I run.

"Yes, ma'am," comes his response over the comms. An engine revs in the background.

I push through the trees, swatting branches out of my way. I'm far enough away from the building now that the guards won't hear me trampling through the belt of oak and maple trees. I burst out of the trees, my shoes hitting the pavement of the parkway. I'm across it in a flash and into the treeline on the other side. My breaths are long and controlled as I pick up speed, weaving through the tree trunks. Water tinkles up ahead, its surface lapping louder as I approach.

I slow as the trees thin, and I can see the green water of the Potomac through the branches. Taking care to move slowly so I don't attract attention, I slip to the river bank and peer up and down its length.

There's a small boat moored to the river's edge fifty yards from my position. Lotus is sitting in the small craft, one hand on the edge, the other on the steering wheel. He catches sight of me through the low windshield and waves.

I break from cover and sprint down the bank, careful not to trip over the tree roots that jut out of the ground. Hopping into the back of the boat, I duck down near the floor long enough to take off my mask, balaclava, and gloves. Then I slide into the passenger seat beside Lotus.

"You ready?" He grins.

"Hell yes."

"By the way, you smell."

Laughing, I slug him in the shoulder.

"Ouch."

"Get us home."

"Yes, ma'am."

The boat engine putters as he steers us away from the bank and down the river. Once he opens her up, it feels like we're soaring over the water like a weightless sea bird over the ocean. I throw my arms out to the sides, embracing the flood of adrenaline that rushes through me, making me giddy with pride. We've done it. We successfully broke into CIA headquarters, and back out again, without getting busted. We're titans of espionage. We're the best in the field. We're definitely going to stop Nexus before he can get his hands on the NOC list or any of the CIA's agent files.

"I'm out," I say, letting my pride tinge my voice. "We did it."

Haru and Julep cheer on the other end.

"That was epic," Lotus says, and then sniffs the air. His nose wrinkles in disapproval. "What did you do? Take a shower in bug spray?"

I can't help but snicker. Lotus has no idea how right he is.

Chapter 29

Lotus drives the whole way to the Ivory Tower with the car window down to cut the smell that permeates my clothing.

At first I find it funny, but after a while the smell starts to give me a headache.

We pull into the parking garage under the hotel and park in our usual spot.

The pop music starts the second we set foot in the Tower. Lotus groans. "I'll never listen to Natasha Day again."

"Maybe we should disable the entire system," I mutter.

Royal is waiting for us in the control room. "Well done. I'm proud of all of you. By the way, COO Harris just called to postpone our exercise. Apparently they're having to fumigate their building."

"What a shame." A glint of triumph plays on my face. "She'll be surprised by the report she's going to get from us, then."

"Indeed." He turns to go, but stops. "Just to let you know, Charles is stopping by in a few minutes. He was in the city and wanted to say hello."

Darnay either has impeccable or terrible timing, but I wisely bite my tongue.

Starling and Clarity burst into the Tower, grinning as they jog toward us. "How did you get out of the vent?" Starling asks, taking in my dirty clothing and mussed hair.

"I'm so sorry I couldn't get you out," Clarity says, putting an arm around my shoulder. But she recoils when she gets a whiff of me. "Wow. That's strong stuff."

"Tell me about it."

Julep comes into the den, looking comfortable in electric blue leggings and an oversized, black hoodie. "How'd it go?" she asks, eyes on Lotus.

He ducks his head coyly. "Like taking candy from a baby."

She grins. "I've got a pot of chicken and wild rice soup going in the kitchen for lunch. Are any of you hungry?" The question is directed to all of us, but she doesn't take her eyes off Lotus.

His gaze rises to meet hers. "Famished."

They meander away down the staircase, hovering a few inches away from each other.

"That sounds delicious," Clarity says, sniffing the air. "I think I'll see if there's enough for me before I change out of these clothes." She winks at me before walking down the concrete staircase herself.

"You did great work today," Starling says, deep brown eyes on me. "I'm chuffed to be working with you." He leans down toward me and whispers conspiratorially. "And I'm looking forward to our date."

"Me too." All too aware of my less-than-pleasant perfume, I take a step back. "I should hit the showers." I skitter past him into the control room, where Haru's hunched over her laptop, typing over the keys while glancing at the image of her home in the lower right corner.

"How's he doing today?"

She gives a "Hmm," in response.

"Here's your thumb drive. It worked like a charm."

Haru takes the drive from my outstretched fingers and pockets it. "Yay! Aren't the graphics pretty? I love them."

A chortle escapes me as I stride down the hall, aching for a shower and a fresh change of clothes. I successfully snuck fake files out of the CIA today, and welcome the bloom of pride in my chest.

A hot shower only bolsters my confidence, but as I step out of the bathroom, the chill in the air smothers it. Heavy silence greets me, making me pause to listen. Something isn't right.

I drop my shower basket in the door of my room, but Clarity's not there. A quick check reveals that Lotus, Julep, and Starling's rooms are also empty. My mouth quirks at the sight of Starling's pest control uniform neatly folded on top of his laundry basket. Haru's room is locked, like always.

I go still in the dormitory hallway, listening for clues as to what's going on. There's nothing.

Crossing my room in a few quick strides, I swipe my tranquilizer gun off my desk. It was sloppy to leave it there rather than stowing it in the armory right away, but I had to get that chemical stink off. It was making my brain hurt.

In slow, precise movements, I creep down the hallway. My gaze searches the den for a hint of my teammates, but I see no sign of anyone. The hooks along the wall are covered with jackets, scarves, and two motorcycle helmets, just like always.

Darnay slinks out of the hallway to the control room, putting on a charming smile when he sees me. "Loveday, I'm told you did a stellar job today. Great work!"

"Thanks," I say, not taking my eyes off him.

"I'd best be off. Toodle-oo."

He exits the Tower without a backward glance.

I'm left alone in the den, and the pall of dread in the air is unmistakable.

It's not until I reach the hall outside the control room that I hear a rustle of movement.

I peek around the corner, and my eyebrows push together in confusion.

Starling, Clarity, and Haru are huddled around her desk, shooting wary glances toward Royal's office door.

Starling catches sight of me out of the corner of his eye and averts his gaze.

Strange.

I shift my weight, and Clarity hears. Turning, she spots me. With one hand, she beckons me forward to join them. "Royal caught Julep and Lotus kissing in the kitchen," she breathes in my ear. "He practically dragged them into his office."

My eyebrows shoot up. "That's not good."

My sister bites her lip, her eyes wide. "No."

The rumble of Royal's voice rising reaches my ears. He's not quite yelling at the two of them, but only just.

"Excuse me," I say, pushing through my teammates and reaching for the door knob.

"Don't!" Clarity says, but I swing the door open, not heeding her warning.

Royal is a tower of rage as he looks at me, blue eyes sizzling and muscles tensed as he stands behind his desk with his hands balled into fists.

On the other side, Julep and Lotus stand shoulder to shoulder, her with her hands clenched at her sides, and he with his arms crossed tightly over his chest.

"Mind if I interrupt?" I ask, swinging my gaze to my dad.

He clenches his jaw. "As a matter of fact, I do. Leave, Loveday."

"I don't think I will." I click the door shut behind me. "This is just as much my team as yours, and I think I should have a say in how it's run."

My dad's face contorts in rage, but he pushes it down, slackening his mouth. "You're still a child."

"Actually, as of yesterday, I'm a full-fledged adult. And in case you haven't heard, a damn good spy."

His hand flies up in frustration and pushes through his sandy brown hair. "You're impossible," he growls.

"Maybe I am," I say, "but whatever you're planning to do to Lotus and Julep, I think you should reconsider."

He opens his mouth to speak, but I plunge on. "This team has been through some exhilarating highs and horrible lows over the past year, and through all of that, Lotus and Julep have been steadfast, reliable, and capable. Not to mention the fact that they're like family to me. I know their relationship is against your policy of fraternization within the team, but I disagree. What's wrong with two people falling in love, as long as it doesn't interfere with their spy work?"

Royal grinds his teeth, still reeking of frustration. "It's dangerous," he growls. "It could compromise them if one of them is hurt in the field, or taken hostage, or worse."

My eyes move from Royal to Julep and Lotus.

Two sets of desperate brown eyes find mine.

"Even if they weren't dating, something unexpected, like a teammate dying, can throw someone off. If I've learned anything in the past year, it's that we have to be prepared for stuff like that. But that's no reason to shut off our emotions. I trust Lotus and Julep with my life. They're good for it."

Julep's mouth curves upward slightly, and Lotus bobs his

head. "Thanks," he mutters.

"And living closed off from your colleagues hasn't done you any favors, either. It wasn't so long ago you expressed regret about not being able to comfort Darnay, your best friend, after his wife died. Am I right?"

Royal opens his mouth to respond, but his phone starts rattling on his desk surface. He exhales roughly. "I have to take this. But we're not through with this discussion." His eyes narrow at Lotus and Julep, and then he gestures with a wave of his hand for us to leave the room.

We file out, and Lotus pulls the door shut behind us. "Whoa, that was intense." He slides his hands into the pockets of his bright red athletic shorts.

Julep swallows. "I've never seen him so mad." She shifts her weight, her shoulder brushing against Lotus's and remaining there.

"What do you think he'll do?" Clarity asks, turning to me.

I shrug. "I don't know, but as far as I'm concerned, this team just pulled off something extraordinary. No matter what he says, each of us belongs here, and I'll fight to keep it that way."

"Did you mean what you said about us being your family?" Julep asks, her gaze steady on mine.

"Every word of it."

She leans forward to embrace me, but the whack of Royal's office door being flung open stops her. The knob crashes into the wall with a metallic smack.

Royal stands over us, wild eyed, the phone still clutched to his ear.

Chapter 30

My dad's blue eyes flash as he looks at me. "Did you download actual files while you were in CIA headquarters?"

My heart slams into my ribcage. "Don't be ridiculous. I wouldn't do that. I used the dummy thumb drive, just like we talked about."

Beside me, Haru blanches, and her entire frame begins to tremble. She looks stunned, as if her mouth is working independently of her control. "I think I'm going to be sick."

She does look a little green.

"That was Gillian Harris," Royal says, holding up his phone. "She says that you accessed the NOC list while you were inside and downloaded the entire thing, along with the rest of the agent files. They're sending someone to take you into custody for questioning."

The blood drains from my head, leaving me woozy. I fling a hand out to steady myself on the desk surface. "What? No! I didn't. I just used the thumb drive…" My words slow as my thoughts pick up speed. "It had a progress bar and a counter. I assumed she'd programmed it that way just for fun…" I spin toward Haru, putting a hand on her arm. "What did you put on that drive?"

She's gone from sickly green to ghostly white. Her tongue runs over dry lips. "I didn't. I mean, someone gave me the thumb drive. He said it was a handy tool he'd used before, but it was harmless. He didn't say anything about it downloading files."

"Who?" Royal crosses the room toward her. "Who gave it to you?"

A flash hits me, and I know. "Charles Darnay."

Starling's jaw drops. "My dad gave it to you?"

Haru nods, mute.

Clarity gasps, and Lotus's eyes nearly pop out of his face. "Wait, Charles Darnay is your—"

"I gave it back to him," Haru whimpers. "I swear I didn't know there were real files on it."

Royal's voice is barely in control when he says, "You're telling me you gave Charles Darnay a thumb drive containing the entire NOC list, and all of the CIA's agent files?"

Tears well in her eyes, threatening to spill over. "Yes."

My heart is pounding in my chest.

Starling staggers, falling into the desk chair behind Haru. "Is he still here?"

By my shocked expression, my teammates know that Charles Darnay is no longer in the Tower. "I talked to him. I could have stopped him, but I didn't know…"

"He stole them," Starling gasps, wiping a hand roughly over his pale face.

Darnay is gone. And so are the CIA's confidential files. There's no telling the damage Darnay might do once he gets into those files.

A low curse slips from my lips.

"Why would he steal the files?" Haru whispers as the tears wash over her cheeks.

My head tilts to the side as I consider this, thoughts spooling through my brain, making connections where before there were none. "I know why."

It explains his unannounced drop in during our mission in St. Petersburg, when we were about to nail The Chin.

Last week's failed security breach at CIA headquarters.

His random and expedient visit, today of all days.

My voice is sure when I speak. "Darnay is Nexus."

Royal's expression is grim as he looks at me. His chin jerks. "No."

But in that instant, I know without a shade of doubt that I'm right. "It makes sense of everything that's gone on over the past year. You have to see that."

Royal looks almost sick when he speaks. "Why would Charles plot a car theft to steal his own files?"

My thoughts fire, looking for an answer. I snap my fingers. "If someone acted on the intel in those files, MI6 would know he was the leak. He had to stage the robbery to cover his tracks."

Starling releases a strangled cry as he leans forward in the chair, hanging his head. "He took advantage of her. My own father. But why would he…?"

Understanding dawns in Royal's eyes. "My god." He rakes a hand through his graying hair. "We have to go. Evacuate the Tower, now!"

Starling jumps to attention.

"We have to get to the kitchen," I whisper, my voice cool. "It's the only exit Darnay doesn't know about."

"We've got bigger problems," Lotus says, looking up from his watch. "Do you know these guys?"

I cross the distance between us and peer down at the screen.

Ten clean-cut men in black suits, white button-down shirts, and black ties are advancing through the underground parking garage toward the service door, guns drawn.

Darnay is at their head.

Resolve runs through my body. "Cobalt Security," I say, clenching my fists.

Lotus's eyes go wide. "Crap."

"Who?" Starling asks.

"Later."

They'll be inside in under three minutes.

My pulse accelerates and my adrenaline kicks in.

"Clarity, Haru, Julep. Get to the kitchen. Push 328756 into the microwave and start climbing."

Haru's eyebrows shoot upward into her bangs, and Julep opens her mouth to clarify.

"We don't have time. Get them out! The rest of us will cover you."

"I have to go back to my room first!" Haru blurts, her voice a squeak.

"What? No, we don't have time."

"I have to! I can't leave the Baron."

My eyes go wide. "Who?"

"My cat," she cries, her cheeks flushing pink.

"You're hiding a cat in your room? That's the weird smell!"

"We don't have time for this," Royal says, his voice harried.

"Fine. Run to your room and get your cat, and I mean run! Lotus, are you armed? Cover her. Clarity and Julep, get to the kitchen and clear our escape route. Once you're out, call the CIA. Let them know what's happening."

I don't have to tell them twice.

Clarity is gone in a moment. Julep slides a handgun out of her waistband and follows. Haru races toward the dormitory, clutching her laptop to her chest.

"Starling, Royal, with me." I bolt down the hall to the armory, slapping my hand against my gun safe door and throwing it open once the panel light flashes from red to green. Swiping my handgun from its place on the shelf, I grab two loaded clips, sliding one into the gun and pocketing the other.

Royal, Starling, and Lotus do the same, arming themselves with their preferred weapons.

"Ready?" Royal asks.

At my nod, he leads us back up the hallway at a creep, his movements practiced and precise.

I slip past him and peek into the den. It's clear.

Haru flies out of the dormitory like the devil is at her heels. There's a pewter gray cat in her arms, and it is huge. This thing must weight twenty pounds, and its bristling fur makes it look even larger. His head swivels toward me and he hisses, his vivid yellow-green eyes shooting daggers.

"Whoa."

"Sorry," she explains. "He's not usually like this, but I woke him up from a nap and…"

My body goes rigid as the security system flares to life, that awful song crooning out of the speakers throughout the Tower.

"Just for tonight, baby, baby, one more dance…"

They've breached the outer security door. In a minute, they'll move into the den in almost impenetrable formation.

Adrenaline runs through me as I set my jaw. This is the moment our training will save us, or break us.

The cat complains with another loud hiss.

"Shh, Baron, it's okay." Haru squeaks, her voice frantic, but the beast appears nonplussed.

"Go!" I order, and the girl clambers down the stairs toward the kitchen, arms wrapped around the furious feline.

With any luck, Clarity and Julep are climbing aloft toward the hotel kitchen already, safe from attack, Haru on their heels.

"Any more surprises you'd like to mention?" Royal says as he levels a weighty look at me. His eyes flick to Starling's face and back again.

"Starling wants to take me out on a date?"

Lotus snorts.

Royal groans. "We'll talk about that later."

The speakers crackle with the sounds of synth-pop and insipid lyrics.

It's not funny anymore.

"Get to the stairs," I whisper to Lotus. "We have to give the others as much time as we can."

Lotus creeps out into the den.

A low rumble vibrates under my feet as the inner door to the Tower slides open, revealing Darnay and his ten goons.

Lotus flings himself into the stairwell as the first shots are fired.

Beside me, Royal leans out just enough to fire off a few shots, trying to pin the enemy down before they can take the den.

Darnay scrambles for cover behind the couch in the den, but the Cobalt forces are held in the hallway.

We've got to keep it that way.

My fingers hover over the trigger. I could put a bullet in Darnay and put him down right now. That couch wouldn't protect him. I take in a sharp breath, slackening my fingers. I can't be responsible for the death of Starling's father. Even though the man has somehow become my archenemy.

Royal ducks as a hail of bullets careens toward us.

The three of us recoil into the hallway.

From across the way, Lotus fires off a few shots. One of the Cobalt guys takes one in the shoulder, and his gun clatters to the ground.

He retreats behind his comrades, cursing loudly.

The Cobalt team returns fire, causing Lotus to scurry for cover farther down the stairs.

Darnay peeps over the couch toward us. "I know it was you, Royal. My best friend."

More bullets spray the concrete walls around us.

I clutch my gun in my hand, firing off a few shots.

It takes a second for the Cobalt guy to register the bleeding wound in his abdomen. One of his comrades pulls at his shoulder, yelling at him to fall back.

"I know you killed her," Darnay yells, his voice rough with anguish.

"What?" I yell, doubting my very ears.

Royal's face drops in sorrow. "I was following an order," he says, his voice breaking. "I didn't know who she was. I'm so unbelievably sorry."

Darnay motions to his men, who send another volley of bullets our way.

My ears are ringing from the blasts. I shake my head, hoping to clear them.

"You killed my Maureen!" Darnay wails.

Starling goes stiff.

The weight of the accusation hangs in the air, pushing down on us like too many blankets, smothering us with hot, stale air.

A jolt like lightning streaks down my spine, and my mouth goes dry. He can't be saying what I think he is. I open my mouth to clarify, but there are no adequate words. My tongue weighs heavy in my mouth as if numb. Behind my ribcage, my heart throbs. My breaths go shallow as my throat constricts. Starling's mom. That's what it's always been about. I just never saw it.

Chapter 31

I'm frozen in place, not sure if I should keep watching the enemy combatants at my front, or shift to a position I can defend against Starling. I don't know what he'll do with this new revelation, but I won't risk my dad's safety.

I can't believe it's come to this—a choice between blood and heart—but if Starling tries to turn his gun on my dad, I'll shoot him. Even if it's the most difficult thing I ever do. Even if the blood never washes off my hands.

A beat passes, but Starling doesn't lower his weapon. And he also doesn't turn it on Royal. Instead, he works his jaw, his eyes glazing over in shock.

The Cobalt team fires more rounds at us, their bullets crashing into the walls. Gray dust and bits of concrete litter the floor.

Coughing, I pull my shirt front up to cover my nose and mouth.

"Surrender," Darnay calls, voice ringing with fury, "and I'll let the rest of your team go. I'll make your punishment quick."

Royal considers this.

"You can't do that," I whisper-yell at him. "He'll kill you, right here, right now."

"I killed his wife," he responds.

"Under orders! That's not your fault. We're soldiers, remember?"

His piercing blue eyes flit to mine for a split second before returning to our attackers.

Leaning out from the wall, I fire, managing to hit two of the Cobalt guys in the chest.

They retreat, leaving six more in their wake.

Six more.

Deep breaths.

We can do this.

Lotus fires, sending the Cobalt guys ducking back into the hallway.

"Are you with us?" Royal asks, and I know the question is for Starling, even though his eyes are focused down the hall toward the men in black.

Starling gulps, his breath coming in pants. "Yes, sir."

Royal's voice drops even lower. "I want you to know, I'm deeply sorry."

Starling gives a quick nod, but the sorrowful expression on his face rends my heart into bleeding shards. This business has cost so much. How much more will we be asked to pay?

Royal rests a hand on my back. Leaning forward, he whispers in my ear. "At the next break in the fire, Starling and I will lay down cover. You get to the kitchen."

I start to argue, but his cold look stops me.

Biting my lip, I give a slight nod.

When there's a pause in the shooting, Royal and Starling fire their weapons toward the Cobalt guys, who hug the walls for some semblance of cover.

I sprint out of the hallway and leap across the den, barreling into the stairwell.

Gunfire blooms around me, and something bites into my thigh.

I ignore it, high from the adrenaline, my blood roaring in my ears.

Lotus creeps forward to steady me. "Go," he says. "We can handle this."

My instinct is to stay. Argue. But I ignore it. Instead, I hobble down the stairs, the soles of my shoes slick on the floor. I slip, my fingers grazing the cold cement. Confusion clouds my mind. Why the sudden bought of clumsiness?

I reach down to itch on my thigh, and my hand comes back covered in deep red blood. My blood. I bobble, grabbing for the wall with my hand. A crimson handprint smears streaks along the wall as fumble toward the microwave.

More gunfire from above makes me speed on, limping as quickly as I can manage.

Is this what it feels like to be shot? Like a film has lowered over me, rendering me numb?

Adrenaline surges, urging me onward.

Reaching up, I smack myself in the cheek, hoping the haze will clear.

It works, for a few seconds.

I stagger across the kitchen, dragging my injured leg. My shoes struggle to find purchase on the slick floor, almost sending me sprawling.

Panic flickers to life in my belly. I have to get out of here.

There's a gaping hole above the microwave where my teammates lifted themselves into the air vent.

Grappling with the edge of the countertop, I try to hoist myself onto the concrete surface. My injured leg smacks on the drawer pull and stars flash in my eyes. Slapping myself in the cheek does nothing to clear my head this time.

I'm panting now, listening to the gunfight raging above me with increasing dread.

The crackle of a flash bomb igniting above raises goosebumps along my arms.

Feet scurry across the floor, but I can't tell whose they are.

There's a lull in the battle, gunshots giving way to coughing and shouting.

A crunch as flesh meets bone.

Who's winning?

There's no way to know.

Behind me, strong arms lift me up onto the counter. "Let's get you into that air vent."

It's Starling, his warm breath fanning the skin at the back of my neck.

I glance over my shoulder and melt in relief.

Lotus is there, and so is Royal, although there's a bullet wound in his arm.

"How, how did you…?"

"Not now," Royal says. "We have to keep moving."

I nod, shoving my gun into its holster and reaching up with trembling arms toward the first rung of the ladder that's hidden inside the air vent. I pull myself up, wincing as some of my weight presses down on my injured leg, but I keep climbing.

Beneath me, Starling whispers words of encouragement that I can't make out through my clouded mind, but the constant murmur is comforting.

I'm almost to the top, three rungs from escape.

My bloody hand slips, and I barely catch myself.

"You're almost there," Royal calls from below. "You can do this."

My chest is heaving and my head is swimming as I reach the platform. Gathering what little strength I have left, I fling myself over the edge, and fall into the hotel's walk-in deep freeze.

My vision tunnels, and the scuffling around me quiets as if it's miles away.

I fight to return to the light, but my leg pulses in agony. Everything goes fuzzy.

The next minutes are blurry. Images of my teammates solidify for a moment then fade. I'm carried, jostling in another's arms, into a darkened box. I'm laid down in the shadow, and figures move past me, careful not to bump into my prone form.

Lights flicker into the dark at regular intervals, through a window up ahead. I think we're in a vehicle, but I can't focus past the pain in my leg.

Someone presses a hand to the bullet hole, making me yell a string of curses. Searing pain shoots up my body from the pressure on my wound. Grinding my teeth, I hold back another cry of anguish.

"It's okay, we've got you," Julep says.

"Where are we going?" Clarity shrieks.

"Just around the corner," Royal responds in a harried tone. "Stop!"

Lotus brings the vehicle to an abrupt halt. "What now?"

"Give me two minutes."

"We may not have that kind of time," Starling says, his large hand on my shoulder.

"I can't leave her." Royal jumps out of the car and slams the door behind him.

Another pain cuts through me, and I can't stop myself from gasping.

"Shh," Clarity moans, squatting beside me and stroking my hair. "Try not to move. We're getting you some help."

Black tunnels my vision, and my sister's voice fades. I'm going to pass out again. But instead of fighting it, I leap into the dark, and let go.

Chapter 32

A slow vibration enters my awareness, lifting me into consciousness.

Gentle fingers comb through my hair.

"Clarity?" I mumble, the word barely audible through my dry mouth.

There's a rustle of movement above my head.

Is someone about to attack me? Am I still in the Tower?

My eyes pop open. I'm lying on a yoga mat in the back of a large vehicle. The lack of windows along the car's body confuses me. It's not Royal's van. The inside walls are spattered with flecks of paint in a myriad of colors, adding to my confusion. I squint into the dark.

My teammates are hunched in the space around me, watching.

"Whose van is this?" My words come out hoarse and brittle. I lick my lips to moisten them.

"Carl, the maintenance guy. I hotwired it." Lotus's expression is sheepish in the rearview mirror.

"Won't he miss it?"

"We'll worry about that later." I've never seen Royal's face so ashen.

"What happened?"

"You passed out, sis."

A shudder of recognition runs through me.

Charles Darnay. Cobalt Security. Fiery pain in my thigh.

My breath quickens as I try to push up into a sitting position, but a sharp, burning pain shoots up my leg into my core. "Ow!" I growl.

"Lay still, Loveday. You're safe now." I recognize the soothing feminine voice. Looking up, I catch sight of a soft, pale face peering down at me. It's Truly.

"Hi," I whisper.

She smiles.

I twist just enough to find the woman herself sitting with her back against the driver side of the van, her legs stretched out across the floor. Her hair is an unruly puff of bedhead blonde, and she's wearing a fluffy lavender bathrobe over red and black flannel pajama pants. Only her feet are encased in outerwear: rain boots.

Lifting her hand to grip the lapels of her robe, she smiles. "There wasn't much time."

Across from me, Royal clears his throat. "Sorry about that."

Truly's smile warms at this, and her eyes fall to her lap, where she brushes her fingers over the soft terry cloth with her free hand.

"Are you okay?" Clarity asks, scrabbling over Royal's feet to get to me. She rests her hand on my uninjured leg. "You scared me."

I lick my lips again. My entire body feels tight with dehydration. "Does anyone have any water?"

From the front of the van, Julep tosses a steel water bottle to Clarity, who catches it in one hand. Turning, she hands it to me.

I take several deep gulps, but still feel dried out.

"You passed out just as you climbed out of the escape hatch," my sister says. "There was blood all down your leg, so I knew you'd been hurt. I wasn't sure what to do…"

"Starling scooped you up and carried you to the van," Haru adds with a sigh. "It was so romantic."

Julep chuckles, but even in the dark I can feel Royal's features tighten.

"Sounds like it," I say with sarcasm. "Nothing like being shot to inspire the feels."

"I thought you were dead," Starling says. "I thought we'd lost you." His eyes shine in the shadows.

"I'm not that easy to get rid of."

Lotus speaks from the driver seat. "What's our next move?"

Royal rises to his knees to peer out of the windshield. "Look for a secluded place to stop. We need to finish patching up Loveday's leg."

Lotus nods, sitting forward and gripping the steering wheel.

Then my dad turns to me. "We stopped the bleeding, but we've got to remove the bullet and do some proper bandaging. We've got antibiotics, but not much pain medication." His expression is grim. "And this is going to hurt."

"Shouldn't we find a doctor?" Starling asks.

Royal twists to look at him. "There's a doctor where we're going, but we've got to do something about her leg now. It can't wait."

"Do what you have to do." I swallow, bracing myself against the coming onslaught of pain.

Chapter 33

We've been in the van non-stop for hours when finally Royal instructs Lotus to pull off the highway onto a country road that doesn't seem to lead anywhere. He maneuvers the van expertly down the bumpy, pockmarked asphalt, not taking his eyes off the way ahead.

It must be 03:00 or 04:00, the darkest time of night, and there aren't any streetlights along the road, so all I can see is the few feet in front of the van illuminated by its high beams.

Looking down at my leg, my fingers move over the white bandage around my left thigh. Thanks to the pain meds Royal gave me, it doesn't hurt as much. But the dull throb is still there. Sitting still while Julep cleaned my bullet wound is easily my least favorite thing that has happened since I became a spy. I was biting down on my teeth so hard my jaw is sore.

In the intervening hours, my teammates have shuffled their positions in the van, trying to maintain some semblance of comfort. Royal is wedged between the driver and front passenger seats, directing us to wherever the heck we're going. Truly has fallen asleep with her head against the back door of the van, and bounces every time we hit an uneven spot in the road. Haru, too, is asleep, her giant cat sprawled on the metal floor by her side.

Near the mattress where I'm reclining, only Clarity and Starling are awake.

Clarity's reading on her tablet, her eyes lit by the device's low glow.

Starling sits opposite me, arms slung over his raised knees. Catching my eye, he shifts onto his hands and knees.

My stomach flips as he crawls toward me, our eyes caught in the dark.

He sinks down right beside me on the mattress, a mere breath away. Stretching out, he lets his feet hang off the edge so they dangle over the metal floor. "How are you feeling?" he whispers.

"Not great."

"I'm sorry." His shoulder brushes mine and doesn't move away.

Exhaling a deep breath, I lean into him. "Thanks, for pulling me out."

Sending a covert glance toward my dad, Starling slides his hand along the mattress and up into my lap, where he settles it over both of mine.

I feel warm and liquid at his touch.

"I'm so relieved you're going to be okay," he whispers, and his warm breath caresses the top of my head.

"Me too."

He squeezes my hands again.

I almost ask him not to let go. I'm not ready to break contact.

But he doesn't remove his hand.

I'm starting to feel sleepy again, my eyes heavy. I open them wide, trying to ward off the fatigue.

Clarity swipes at her screen, absorbed in her book.

"Royal?" Lotus asks from the driver seat. "I think we're being followed."

Sure enough, the high beams of a car approach behind us, reflecting off the side mirrors.

Goosebumps cover my arms, making me shiver.

"Take your time, but make the next turn. See if they follow us."

Lotus nods, shifting in his seat.

The rest of us fall into a hushed silence.

My stomach twists. If we're attacked, we'll be in trouble. I don't know how much ammo the rest of my teammates have, but if their clips are as light as mine, we'll be in bad shape. Plus, I'm not even close to top form. My team will be a gun down in unfamiliar territory, with nowhere to run.

The van slows and eases into a right turn, plodding through the inky black. Seconds pass without the sound of a pursuing car.

I draw in breath, thinking we're clear.

But then the van's rear mirrors light up, signalling that the car behind us has also turned.

My heart speeds, and I grip Starling's hand tighter.

With his free hand, the boy next to me eases his gun from its holster.

Up at the front, Julep and Royal are doing the same. Julep lights up the flashlight on her phone just for a moment, checking her ammo.

"Take the next left," Royal says.

Lotus runs his hands along the steering wheel, lips pursed. "Yessir."

My pulse speeds, and I try to shift my injured leg, testing its strength. Punishing pain cuts through my muscle, making my body tense. I curse under my breath.

Starling looks down at me in the dark, his gun pointed safely down and away. "I'll protect them," he whispers. "And you."

Again the large vehicle slows, and Lotus turns the wheel, navigating our car to the left.

My team takes a collective inhale, sucking in our breath in anxious anticipation.

A cold sweat breaks out on my skin, making me shiver.

We wait, but there's no light. No sound of a pursuing car.

I exhale loudly, relief flooding through me.

Up front, Lotus smiles. "We're in the clear."

Royal sits on his heels, peering out of the windshield, saying nothing, but the tension inside the vehicle is waning.

My head presses against the metal wall behind me and I close my eyes.

"Try to sleep," Starling whispers. "I'll be here when you wake."

A half smile plays on my lips as my eyes slide closed.

I manage to sleep, despite the jostling of the van, my awareness fading in and out.

It's the barking of several large dogs that snaps me awake and sends my fingers flying toward the holster at my waist.

"Shh, it's okay," Starling says from where he's kneeling in front of me. "We've just arrived."

"Where are we?" I rasp.

"I have no idea," he replies. "Let's have a look."

Truly scoots over so Starling can unlock the van's back doors, and he swings them open.

Two huge black dogs lunge toward us, barking and snarling.

I rear back, making my leg shout with pain.

There's a short hissing sound outside the van, and the two dogs stop their attack in an instant. Turning, they disappear around the side of the vehicle.

I peer out the back, eyes wide, but can't see much in the dark. There's a light source to the left, out of my view.

Royal lumbers past me on his knees and steps out of the van. He, too, disappears to the side.

Truly slides out behind him and follows, tucking her hands into the pockets of her fluffy robe.

Clarity slinks past me in the shadow, and she and Starling help me out of the van. They stand on either side of me, supporting my weight as I stumble along after Royal.

To our left, there's a wide, two story farmhouse with a wrap-around porch.

Out front, there's an elderly man with a solemn expression on his face. A shock of white fluff on top of his head is all he's got left of his hair, and his face is criss-crossed with deep wrinkles. The two dogs sit at attention on either side. "Royal," he says in a stern voice. "Let's get everyone inside, then you can explain the reason for your visit." He turns to Lotus and Julep, who are standing near the van, watching with wary expressions. "You'd best pull the van into the barn."

"It's behind the house," Royal adds.

Lotus nods. "Yes, sir." He and Julep climb into the van and pull it around the side of the house into the night.

"My daughter is injured," Royal says, beckoning me to him.

With the help of Clarity and Starling, I limp forward to stand beside my dad.

"Let's go in, and I'll have a look at her." The man turns and leads the way into the house.

Once we're all inside, minus Lotus and Julep, the older man turns off the porch light and goes about locking the five locks along the door's edge with precise, practiced movements.

I scan the room, noting the low light from dimmed lamps, the roaring fire in the huge brick fireplace along the wall, and the shelves and shelves of books.

"Through here," the man says, gesturing toward the hallway that leads off to the right. "Follow me."

The home must be old, because the hallway is narrow and poorly lit. The walls are lined with old, older, and ancient photographs, beginning in grainy color and ending in grainy black and white.

Royal follows behind, not saying anything.

White hot pain courses through my leg at every step, but I keep pushing forward.

The man turns into a room on the left side of the hall and flips on the light switch.

My eyes take a moment to adjust in the bright light. When I'm done blinking I find myself in what looks like a patient room in a modern health clinic. One wall is lined with blue cabinets, each labeled with a list of medical supplies. On the opposite wall, an exam table with a touchpad control board sits waiting in the reclined position.

"Have a seat," the man says, patting the chair abruptly.

"Wait, who is this?" I ask, gasping at the pain that comes when I twist to meet my dad's eyes.

Royal's eyes move from mine to our host's and back. "This is Dr. Faraday. He's an old friend."

"What he means to say is that I used to patch up Royal and his boys when they got injured in the field, just like I'm going to do with you."

A knock sounds from outside, making me jump.

"That'll be your friends," Dr. Faraday says, moving past us down the hall. The sounds of the locks unbolting comes down the hall, and then Julep and Lotus's voices are added.

"Where is everybody?" Lotus asks, a wary note in his words.

"Just down the hall, there," Dr. Faraday responds. "Follow the light."

Lotus and Julep pop their heads in the door, relief on their faces. "There you are," Julep says.

My teammates crowd the doorway.

"Right, let's get a good look at you," Dr. Faraday says, stepping to the sink and washing his hands thoroughly with lots of foaming soap. "Can't be too careful," he says when he sees me watching him.

"I'll check on Truly," Clarity says before disappearing down the hall.

With a snap, the doctor pulls on bright green latex gloves. "Let's see now…" With gentle fingers he unwraps the bandage around my thigh and gives it a slight poke.

I wince, gritting my teeth.

He laughs. "Sorry about that. I'll just give you a little something and we'll fix you right up." He opens one of the upper cabinets, retrieving a small glass bottle and a syringe sealed in plastic. Unwrapping it, he draws some medication out of the bottle. "You'll be right as rain in just a bit."

Royal stands at my side, his hand a steadying weight on my shoulder.

Julep's phone vibrates. She takes it out of her pocket and glances at the screen. Her face tightens. With a glance at Lotus, she steps forward and whispers in Royal's ear. When he shakes his head, she holds her phone up so he can see the screen. His frown deepens. "When did this happen?" he whispers.

"It was just posted. All the news sites are picking it up."

He curses in frustration.

"What's going on?" I ask.

Royal pauses, and I speak before he can say otherwise. "Don't try to shield me. We're a team. We're in this together; all of us."

He meets Julep's gaze and gives a slight nod. "Show her."

Julep turns the phone toward me so I can read the headline scrawled across the screen:

Mutilated Body Found Outside CIA Headquarters; Terrorism Suspected

"A body? I don't understand."

"They've identified it as a CIA communications officer. I knew him. He was the one who relayed the order to eliminate a woman in a park in the Philippines, eighteen years ago."

My stomach clenches. "Darnay killed him."

"It looks that way."

"But why would he do that?" Julep asks, running nervous fingers through her braids.

"It's a message," Royal says. "I think Charles is determined to retaliate against all of the people who were involved in the killing of his wife. I don't know if I can blame him." These last words are barely a murmur.

"You can't blame yourself."

He shakes off my attempt at consolation.

"Who else was involved in that operation?" Julep asks, trying to keep us focused.

"It was just me, Bernie, and…" Royal trails off, his eyes flying up to mine.

"And?" Julep prods. "Who gave the order?"

The room goes still, and it feels like an eternity before Royal answers. "Gillian Harris."

Dr. Faraday takes the opportunity to push his needle into my thigh.

I glare at him, but remain still. "A little warning next time, yeah?"

He chuckles. "I find my patients do better if they're focused elsewhere."

"Like hell they do."

Royal shoots a disapproving look at me, and then turns to Julep. "We need to secure Ms. Harris. Call her. Now. Before Charles gets to her."

Julep nods and lifts her phone. She frowns as she waits for an answer. "She's not picking up."

My dad rakes his hand through his hair. "Julep, will you go? I can't leave Loveday."

"No, it should be me. I should go." Starling's voice is edged with anger. "He's my father."

Royal shakes his head. "No, I need you to stay here since Loveday is injured."

A muscle in Starling's jaw clenches. "I'm going. You can't stop me."

The two of them glare at each other, Royal's shoulders bunched in frustration, and Starling's body coiled tight like a jungle cat about to pounce.

Tension fills the air, hushing the noises of the night around us. We wait.

At last, Royal gives the slightest shake of his head. "Go, and take Julep with you."

"I'm going too," Lotus says, shouldering his way into the inner circle.

"No, you're not," Julep snaps.

Lotus swings his attention to Royal, knowing he has the final say.

"Starling and Julep will go."

Lotus growls in frustration, but doesn't press it further.

"Right away," Julep says. They move toward the door.

"Wait." The word is out before I have the chance to call it back.

The two of them turn back to face me, questions in their eyes.

"Be careful, okay?" It's all I can muster at the moment, in front of so many witnesses.

Julep gives me a faint smile and disappears into the hall.

Starling sends a devil-may-care glance toward my dad before striding across the room and pressing his lips to mine in a brief kiss.

And then they're gone.

Haru says, "Aww," but Royal rolls his eyes.

The front door opens and closes. Outside the house, footsteps run by.

A vehicle drives past the building at a steady speed, churning over the hard-packed ground.

"Where are they going?" Clarity cries, running into the room looking panic-stricken.

"To see if COO Harris is safe."

Her eyebrows draw together in question until Royal explains the situation. "So now we wait. Hopefully they find Gillian before Charles does."

Dr. Faraday patches me up before pushing me out into the living room in an old wheel chair, where Truly, Clarity, Lotus, and Haru are huddled around the coffee table with steaming mugs in their hands.

"You're next," he says, patting Royal's uninjured arm. The two of them shuffle back down the hall.

"I made everyone coffee," Clarity says.

"Or hot chocolate!" Haru chimes in from her spot next to Truly on the couch. Her giant beast of a cat is sprawled across her lap, appearing to be asleep. But it emits a low hiss when the older woman shifts her weight. Truly frowns and scoots as far from Haru as she can, her body pressed against the opposite end of the sofa. "Cats normally like me," she shrugs.

Despite the somber vibe in the room, Haru giggles. "No, no, Baron. She's our friend." The cat hisses once more, unconvinced.

From where Clarity sits, perched on the arm of the sofa next to Truly, she frowns into her coffee mug.

The hours drag as Starling and Julep drive back to civilization. They chat with us some over our earbuds, which Haru snagged on her way out of the Tower, but mostly we're silent. There isn't a lot to say.

Finally, they reach the city limits.

"We're five minutes away from Ms. Harris's house," Julep informs us.

"Approach with caution," Royal says. "We don't know what kind of situation you're walking into."

"Yes, sir."

Over the comms, the van's engine cuts. "Follow me," Julep says.

"Yes, ma'am." There's no trace of a tremor in Starling's voice.

"Yes."

Car doors open and close. The faint sound of footsteps on pavement reaches my ears.

"There aren't any lights on inside, but it could be nothing. It's only 05:00." Julep's words are calm and steady.

My instincts hum at this. I'm guessing a woman like Gillian Harris would be up pretty early, but I could be wrong.

"Proceed," Royal says.

"The side gate is open. We're going around the back."

Now my gut is screaming. "This could be a trap."

The click of a firearm being made ready is the only response we get over the earbuds.

"I'm sorry," Starling whispers.

My stomach clenches.

"What are you—?" But Julep's question is cut off by the sickening sound of metal meeting flesh.

Lotus jumps out of his seat. "What's going on?" he cries, voice strangled. "Julep?"

"Is everything all right?" Clarity asks, her voice thready. "Is anyone there?"

There's static, and the line goes dead.

"Starling? Julep?" Haru squeaks, pulling her earbud out of her ear and peering down at it. "It's still on. I don't—"

Lotus whips out his phone and dials. He paces the room as he waits, unable to remain still. "Damnit! She's not answering."

"It's not just you," Clarity whispers, her own phone clutched in a trembling hand. "He's got them, too."

Royal pulls his hands out of the pockets of his slacks. "Or Starling flipped sides." Ever the optimist.

I glare at him, my instincts screaming.

"I warned you that any one of us could break, if the right leverage is applied."

My teeth grind in my jaw. My heart feels like it's being julienne cut paper-thin piece by paper-thin piece. It nearly kills me to say, "Maybe you were right."

"I'll, I'll…" Lotus is wild-eyed and too wound up to speak in complete sentences. Instead, he wrings the air with claw-like fingers.

"Lotus, Clarity, gear up. We're going after them."

Clarity shakes her head. "No."

Royal swivels toward her, an expression of pain on his face. He's not surprised.

Neither am I.

"I can't do this anymore." Clarity wraps her arms around her middle, and her body slumps into Truly as she lets out a sob.

"Shh, it's okay." Truly pulls my sister into her arms and holds her tight while she cries.

"What can't you do anymore?" I ask, holding my breath. I'm pretty sure I already know the answer.

Clarity's large mahogany eyes shine when she looks up at me. "This. Being a spy. I'm not cut out for this."

I wait for the bolt of shock, but it doesn't come. I swallow. "I know."

Her lips quiver as she gains control.

Royal crosses the room and puts a hand on my sister's back. "You don't have to go. You can take some time. We'll handle this without you."

Clarity sobs, her cheek pressed into Truly's shoulder.

Biting my lip, I weight my words. I wheel toward her, putting a hand on her shoulder to get her to look at me. "I need you to help me get them back."

"Loveday!" Truly's tone is admonishing.

I hold up a hand to quiet her, not taking my eyes off my

sister. "After that, I won't ask anymore of you. Can you do that?"

Clarity stares at me for a beat, and then nods her head in the affirmative, quiet tears coursing down her cheeks.

I pat her back between Truly's arms. "Thank you." Pulling my attention away from my sister, I turn to Dr. Faraday. "I don't have much time. Can you make me mobile?"

The doctor's lips press tight. "I wouldn't recommend it," he starts, "but you don't strike me as the type to take it easy."

My lips form a grim line. "Nope."

"Then let's get to work."

I grit my teeth as the doctor braces my leg the best he can. We have to leave here as soon as possible. We have to catch up with Darnay before he hurts Gillian Harris, Julep, or anyone else.

"He won't stop until he gets his hands on me," Royal says.

"Then it's up to us to stop him." My heart pinches at the thought of Julep in danger. We're down, but we're not out. As I look around at my teammates—Clarity, Lotus, Haru, Royal, and Truly—my resolve is set. "Among us, there's already been enough heartache. No one else is losing a loved one to violence. Not if I can help it. We're going to stop Nexus, aka Charles Darnay, once and for all."

"And what about Starling?" Lotus asks, eyeing me. Testing my mettle.

My resolve is set. "We'll deal with it. Full stop."

Acknowledgements

This book was so much fun to write, because secrets I had known about from the very beginning finally came out. I hope that you, the readers, are enjoying the journey as Loveday discovers all of the secrets held by her family. Without each and every one of you, it wouldn't be such a joy to be a writer. So, to my readers, thank you!

This book wouldn't be what it is without my friend, Christina Kobel, who graciously agrees to read my drafts and brainstorm ideas when I write myself into a corner. Thanks, friend!

And to my author friends: thank you for your daily support and encouragement. You make being an author so much more fun!

About the Author

Emily lives in sunny Southern California with her husband and daughters. She started writing in elementary school and continued writing in college, where she earned a degree in creative writing. She often gets ideas for stories from the lives of her friends and family. When she's not writing, she enjoys cuddling with her two dachshunds Nestlé and Kiefer, crocheting, watching television, and enjoying the sunshine with her daughters and their flock of backyard chickens.

To learn more about Emily, visit her website: www.emilykazmierski.com

Printed in Great Britain
by Amazon

42297721R00139